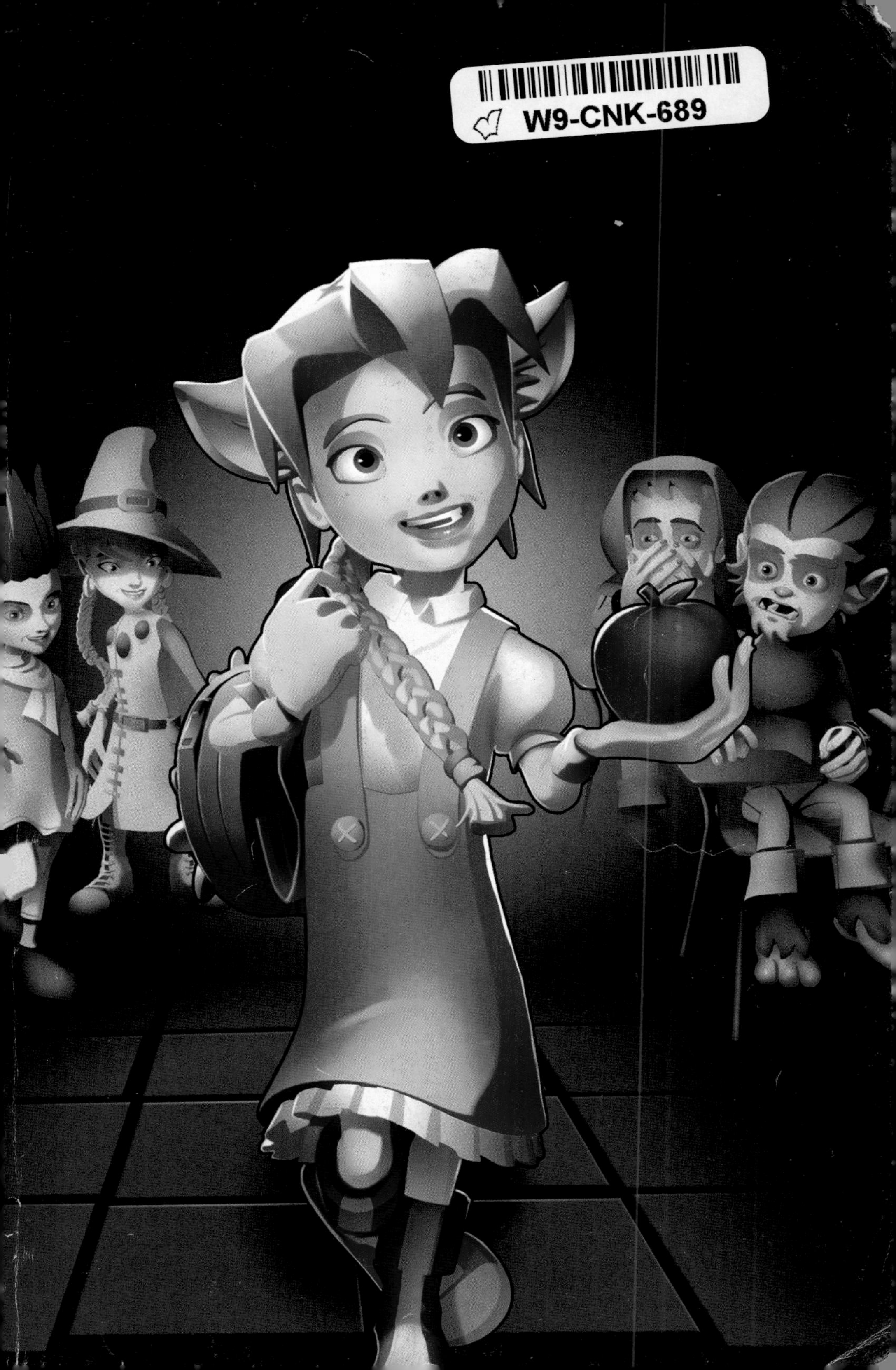

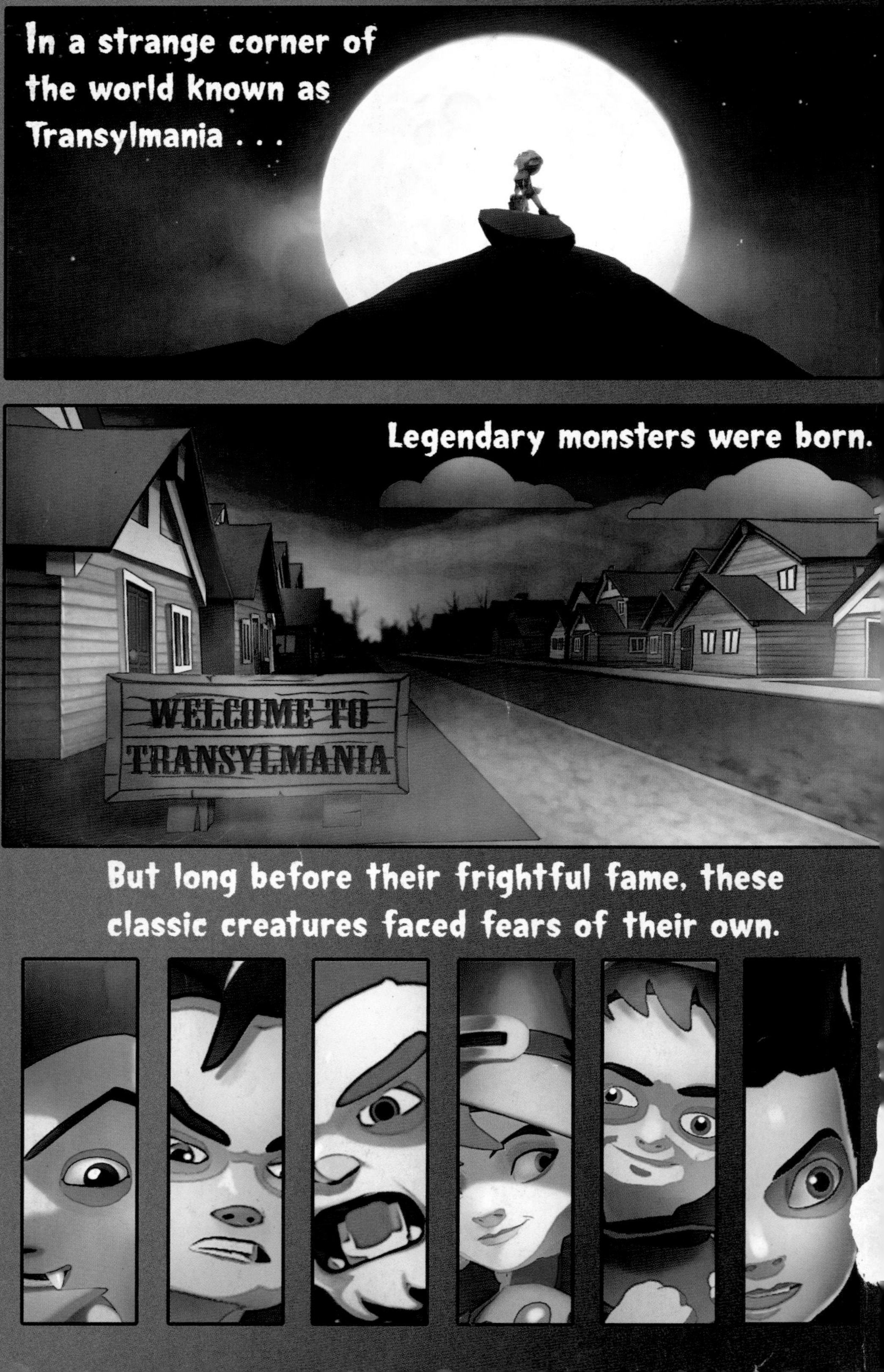
In a strange corner of the world known as Transylmania . . .
Legendary monsters were born.
WELCOME TO TRANSYLMANIA
But long before their frightful fame, these classic creatures faced fears of their own.

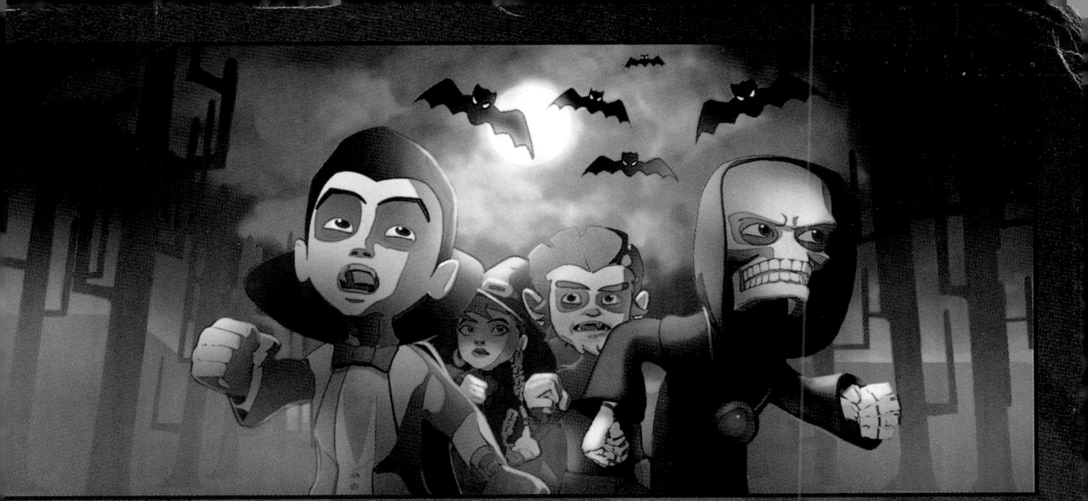

To take on terrifying teachers and homework horrors, they formed the most fearsome friendship on Earth . . .

Mighty Mighty MONSTERS

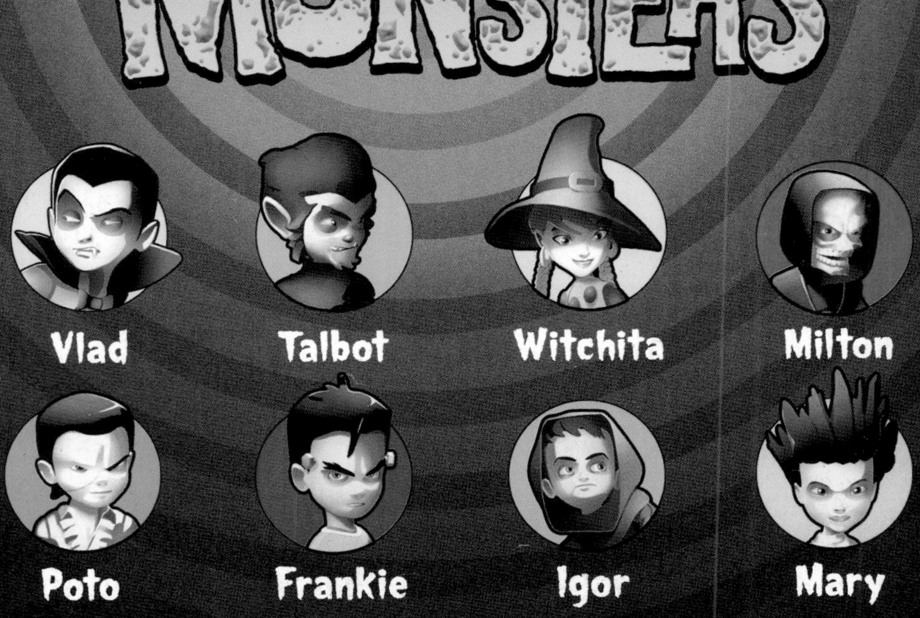
Vlad
Talbot
Witchita
Milton
Poto
Frankie
Igor
Mary

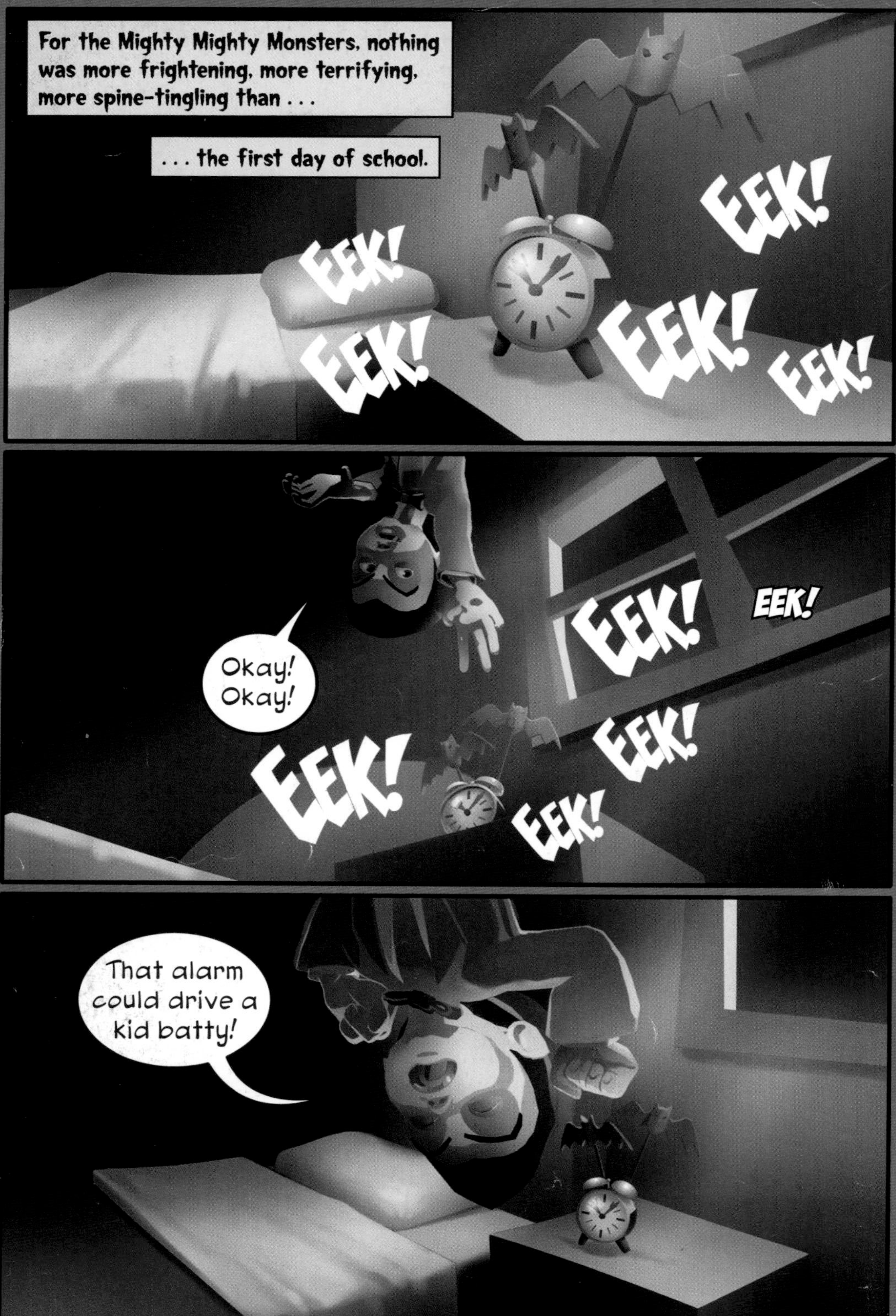
For the Mighty Mighty Monsters, nothing was more frightening, more terrifying, more spine-tingling than . . .
. . . the first day of school.
EEK!
EEK!
EEK!
EEK!
EEK!
Okay! Okay!
EEK!
EEK!
EEK!
EEK!
EEK!
That alarm could drive a kid batty!

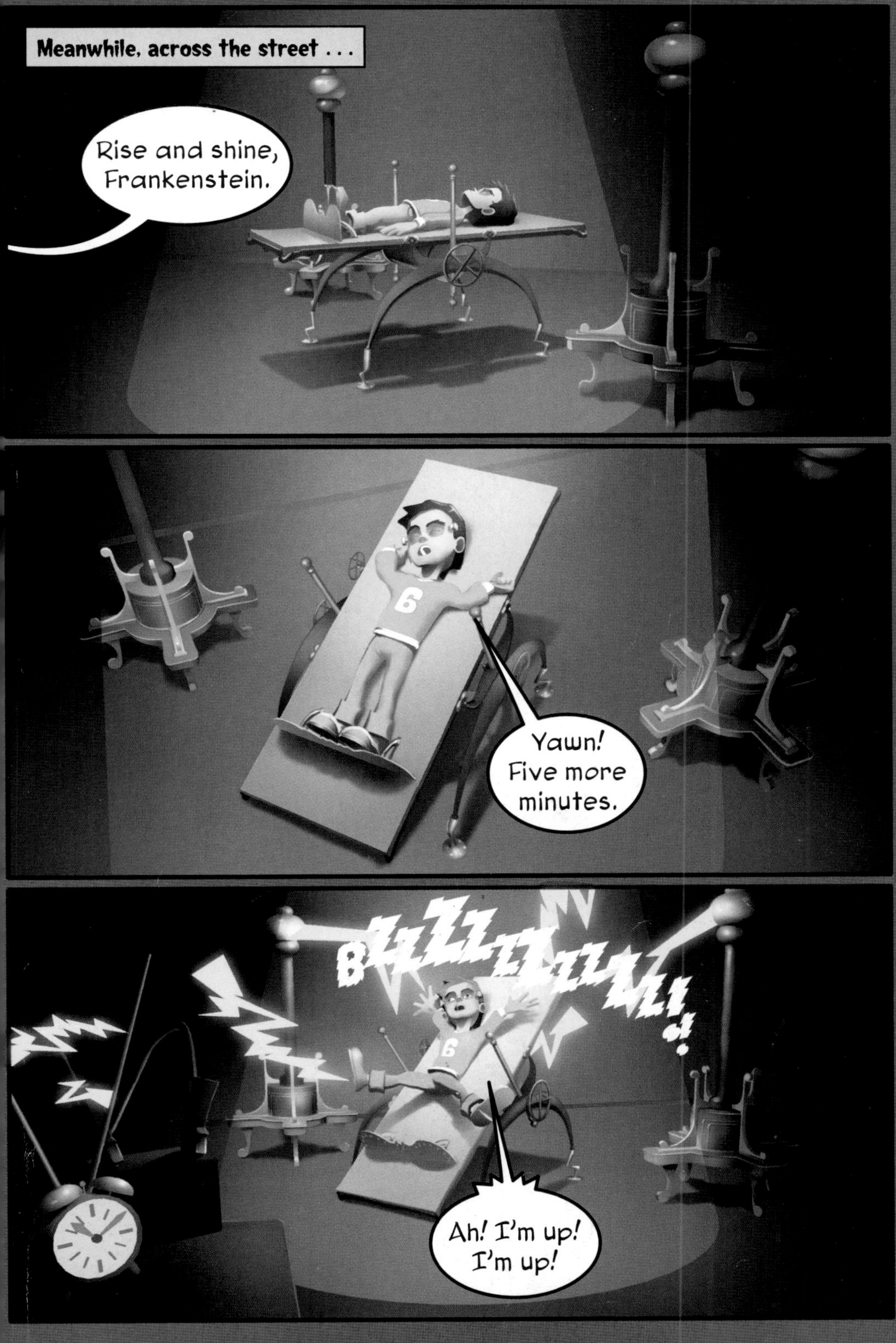
Meanwhile, across the street . . .
Rise and shine, Frankenstein.
6
Yawn! Five more minutes.
BZZZZZZZZZZZZZT!
6
Ah! I'm up! I'm up!

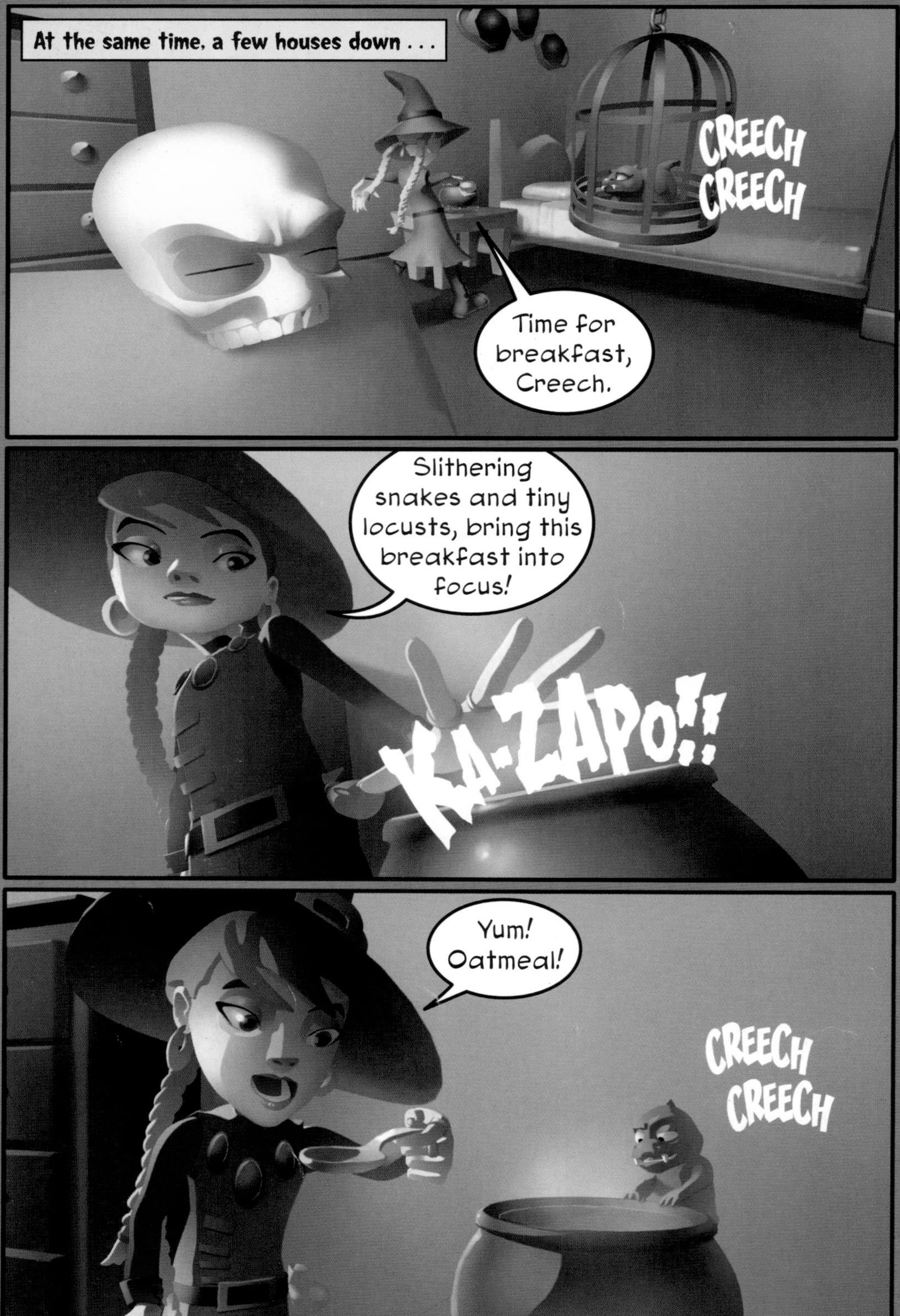
At the same time, a few houses down . . .
CREECH CREECH
Time for breakfast, Creech.
Slithering snakes and tiny locusts, bring this breakfast into focus!
KA-ZAPO!!
Yum! Oatmeal!
CREECH CREECH

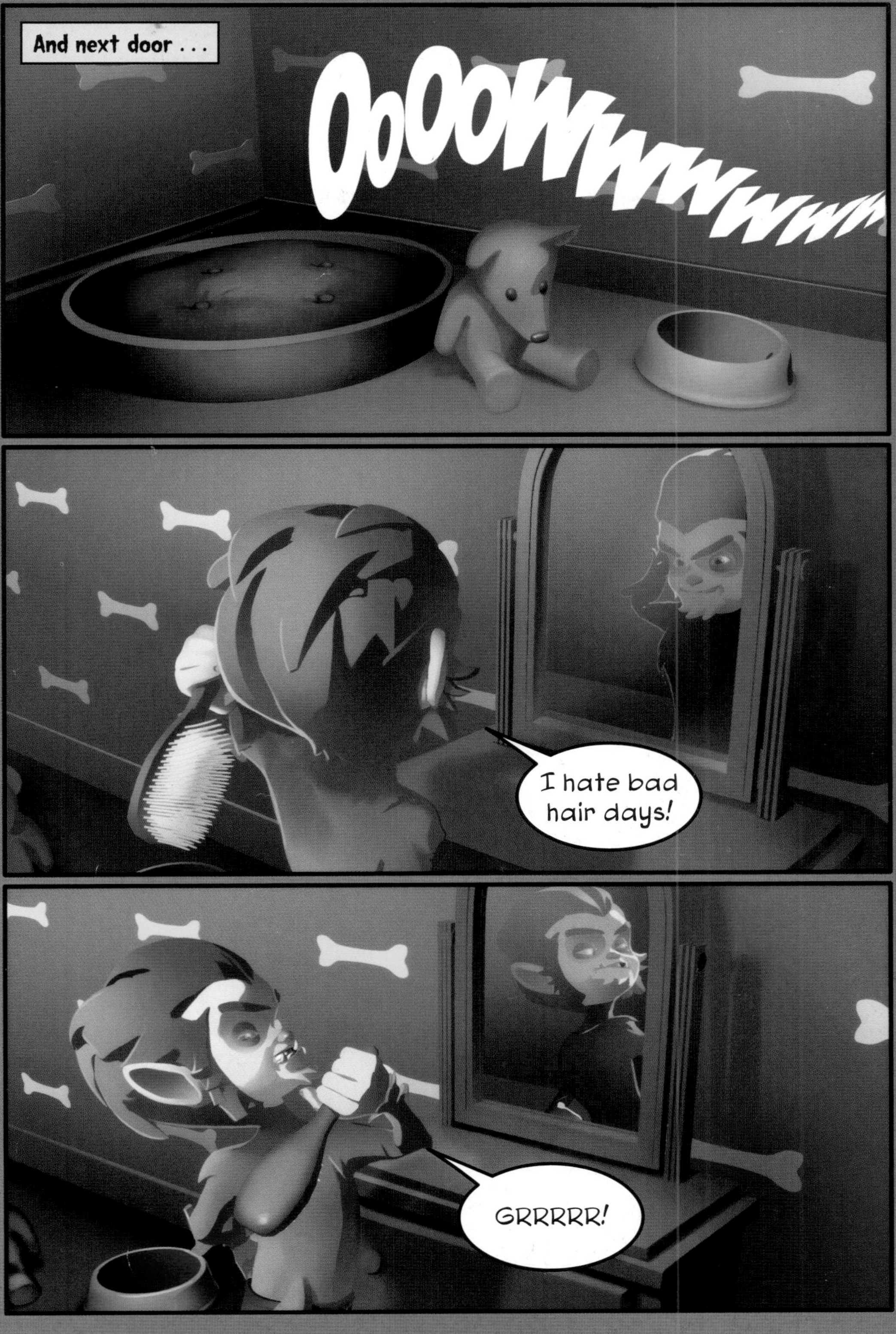
And next door . . .
OoOOWWWWWWWW
I hate bad hair days!
GRRRRR!

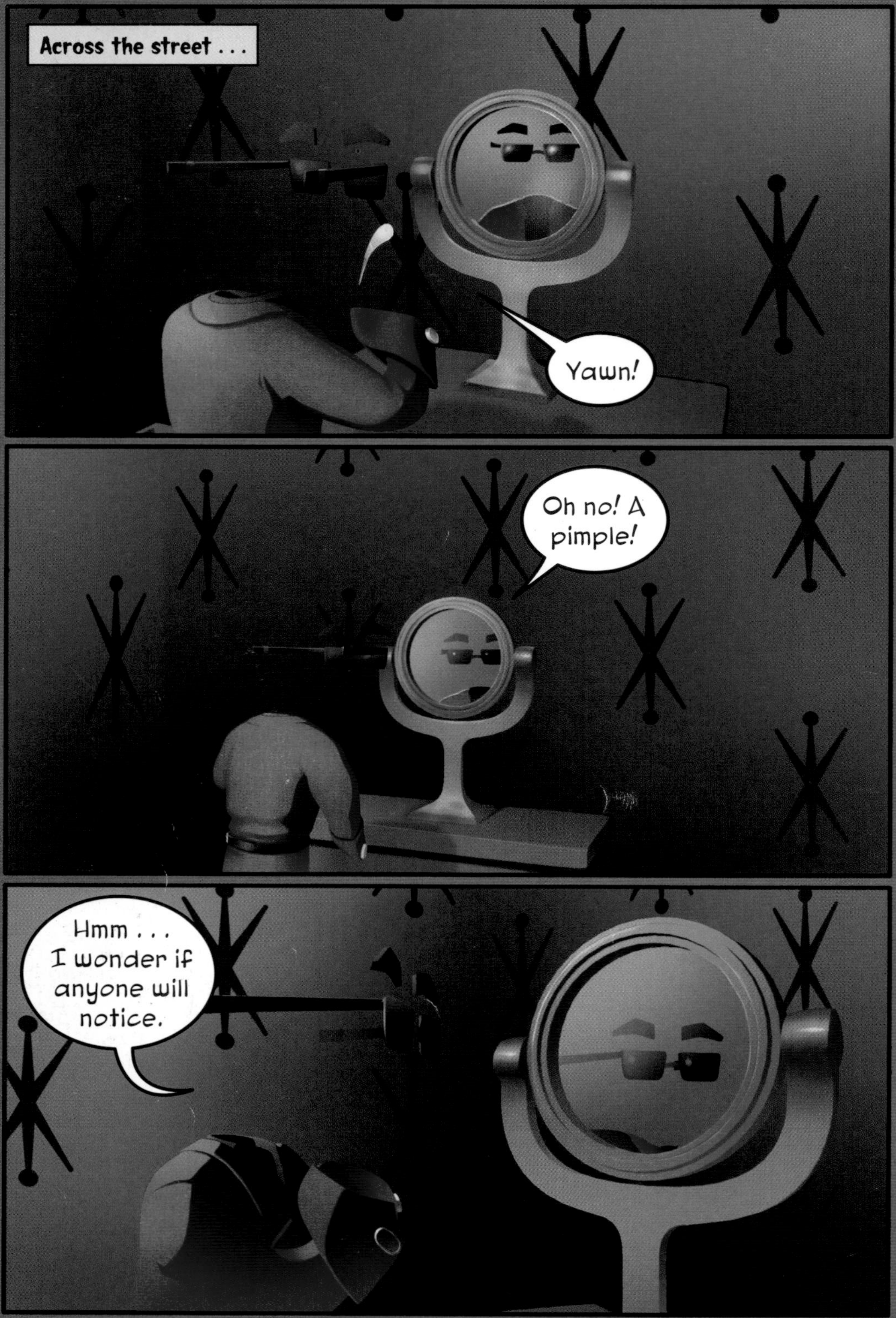
Across the street . . .
Yawn!
Oh no! A pimple!
Hmm . . . I wonder if anyone will notice.

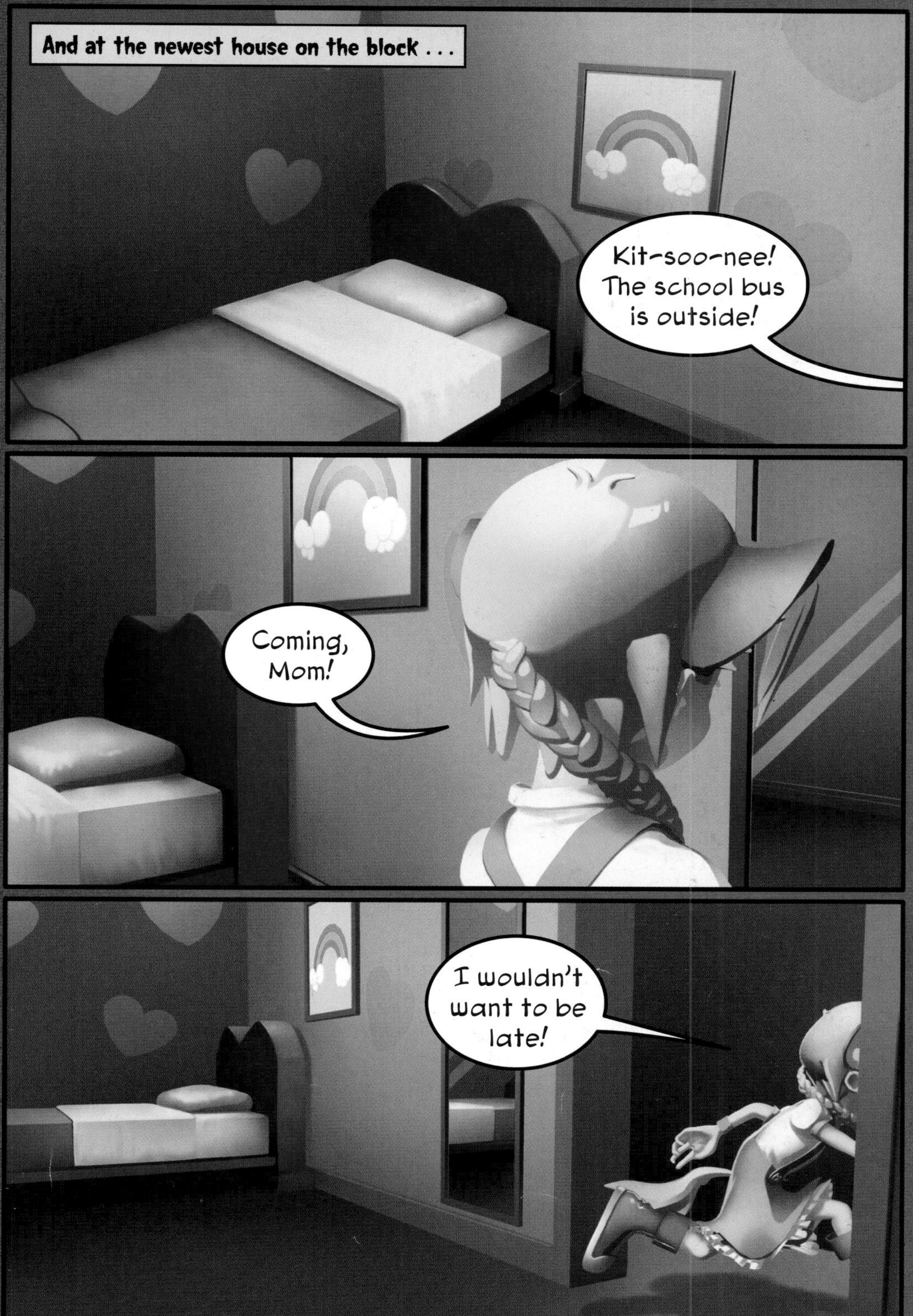
And at the newest house on the block . . .
Kit-soo-nee! The school bus is outside!
Coming, Mom!
I wouldn't want to be late!

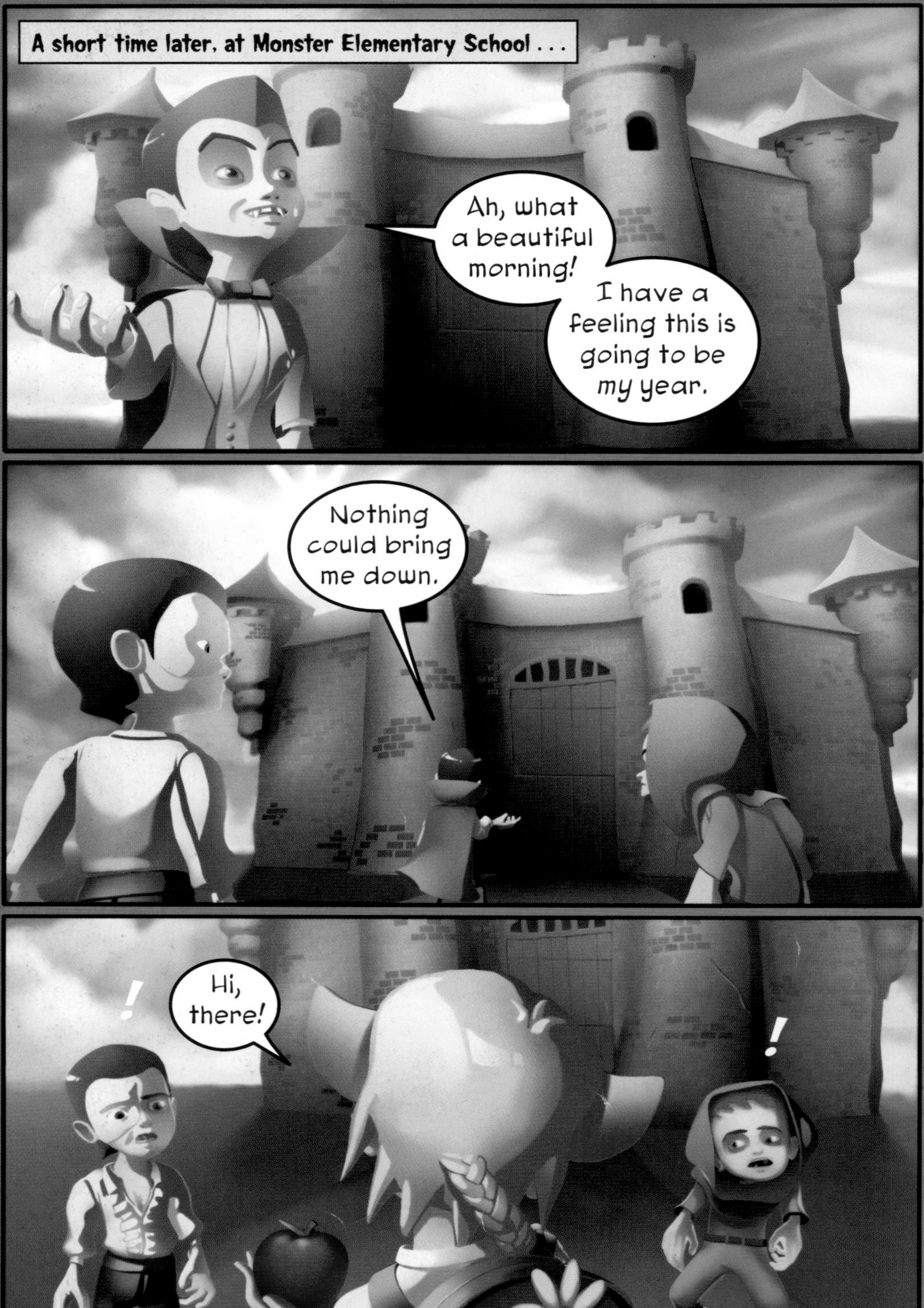
A short time later, at Monster Elementary School . . .
Ah, what a beautiful morning!
I have a feeling this is going to be my year.
Nothing could bring me down.
!
Hi, there!
!

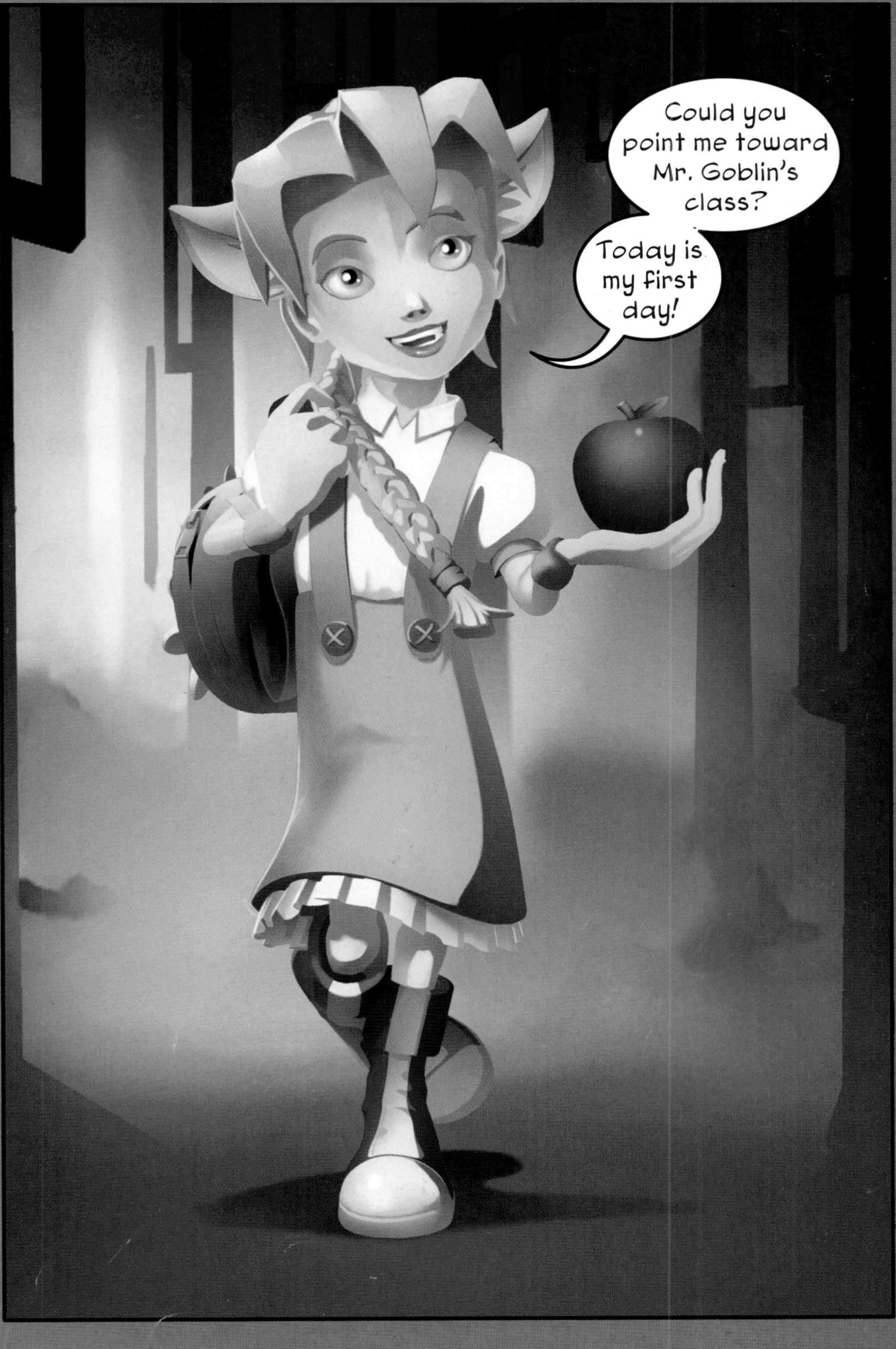
Could you point me toward Mr. Goblin's class?
Today is my first day!

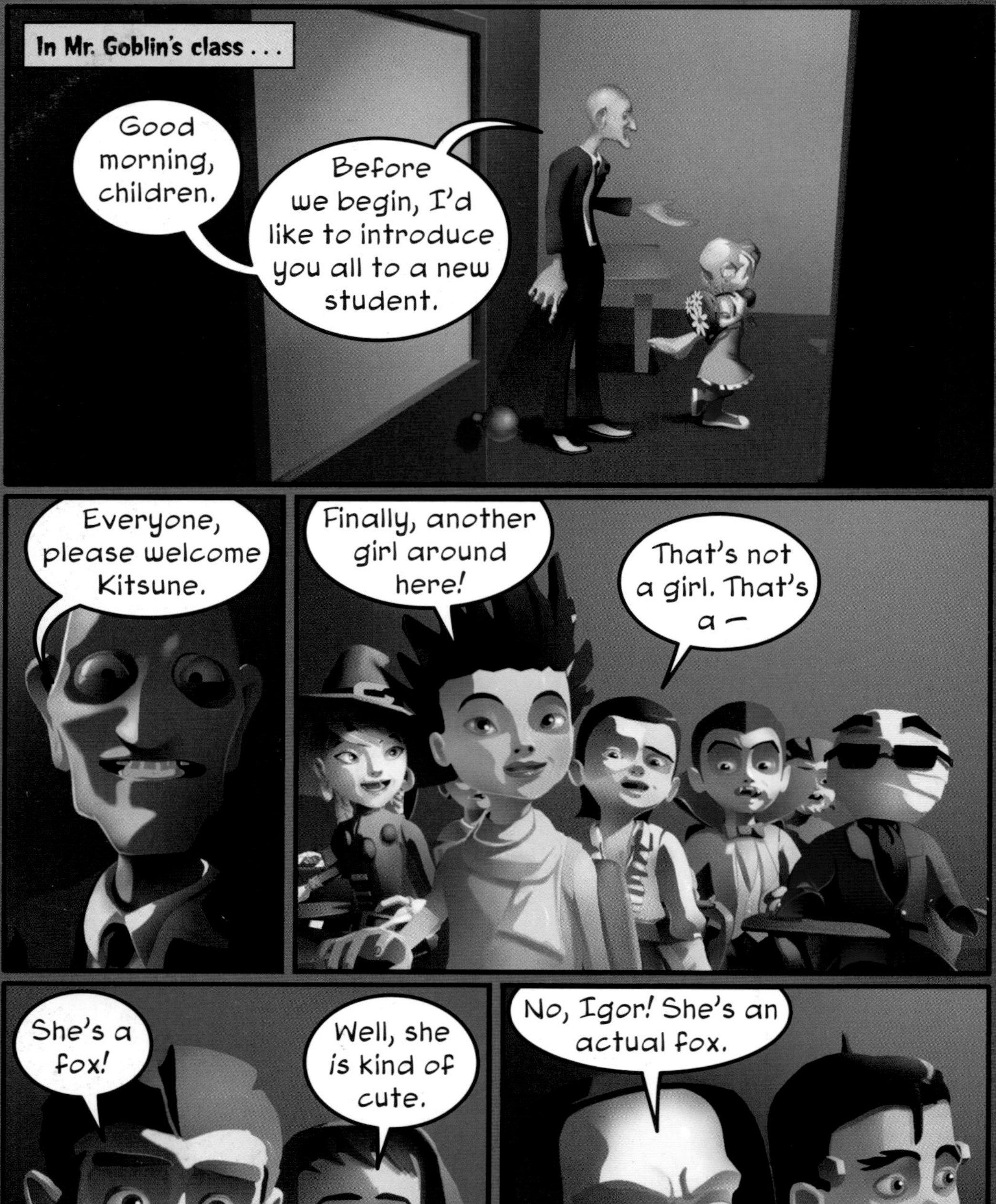
In Mr. Goblin's class . . .
Good morning, children.
Before we begin, I'd like to introduce you all to a new student.
Everyone, please welcome Kitsune.
Finally, another girl around here!
That's not a girl. That's a —
She's a fox!
Well, she is kind of cute.
No, Igor! She's an actual fox.
This is bad.

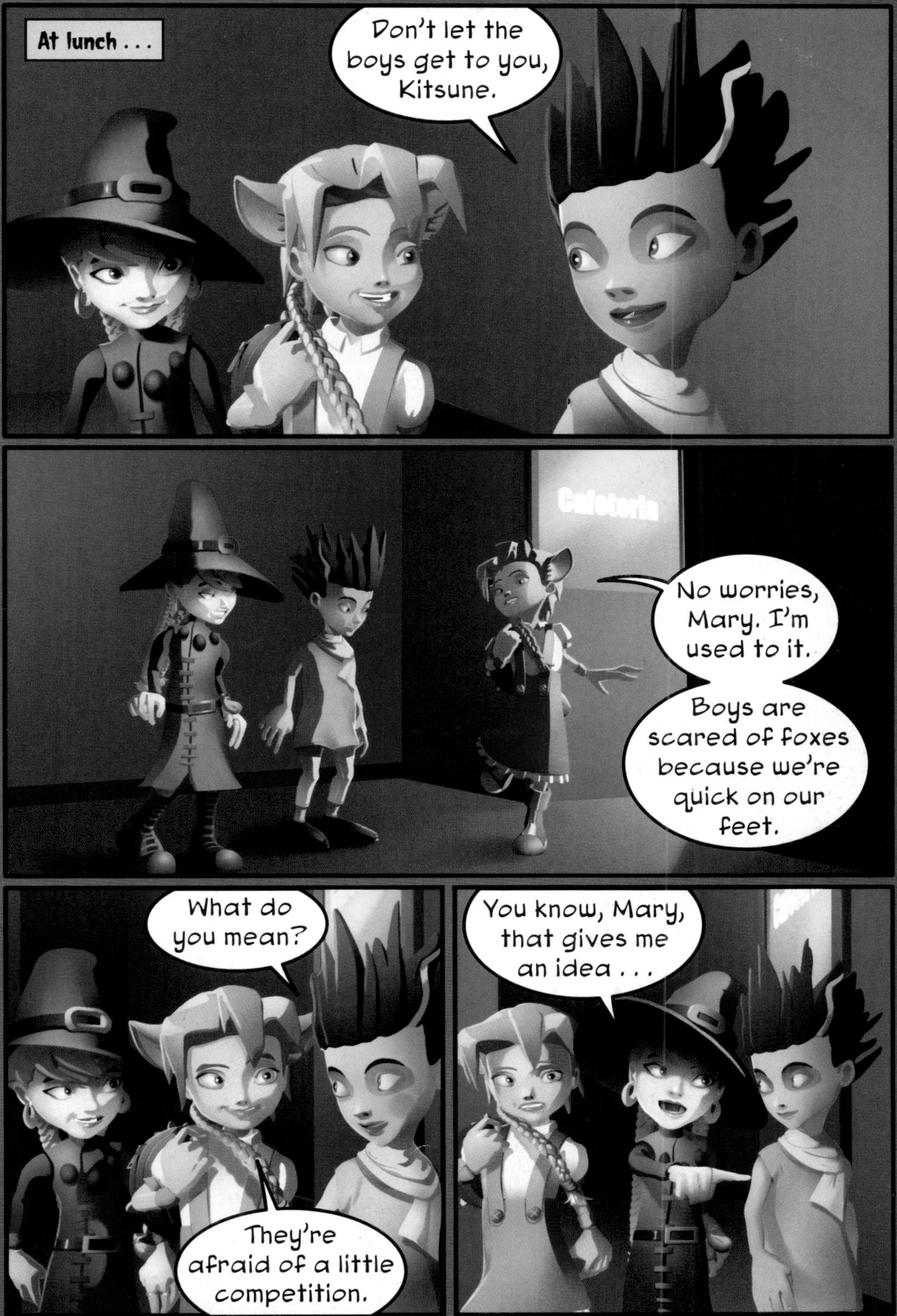
At lunch . . .
Don't let the boys get to you, Kitsune.
Cafeteria
No worries, Mary. I'm used to it.
Boys are scared of foxes because we're quick on our feet.
What do you mean?
They're afraid of a little competition.
You know, Mary, that gives me an idea . . .

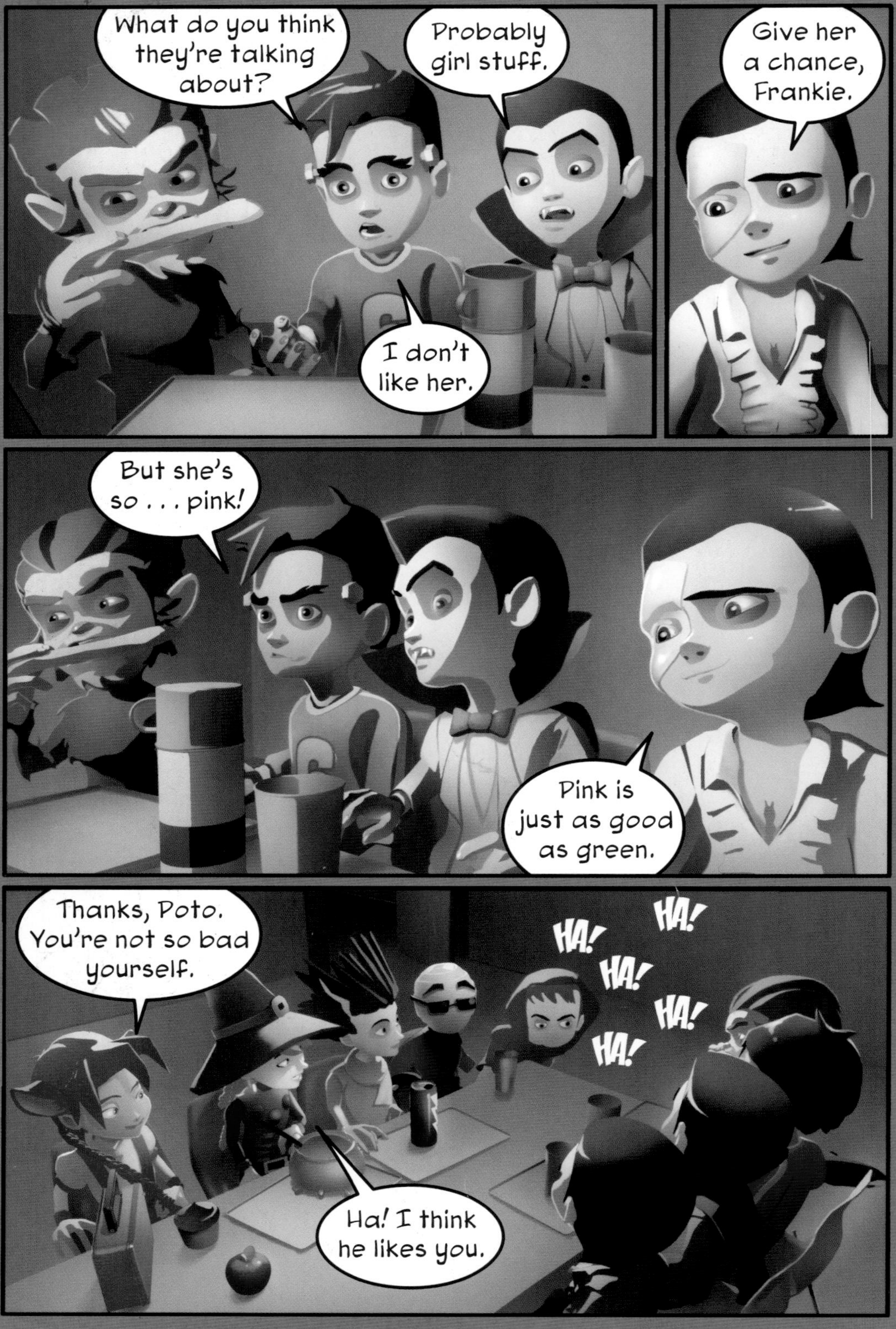
What do you think they're talking about?
Probably girl stuff.
I don't like her.
Give her a chance, Frankie.
But she's so . . . pink!
Pink is just as good as green.
Thanks, Poto. You're not so bad yourself.
HA!
HA!
HA!
HA!
HA!
Ha! I think he likes you.

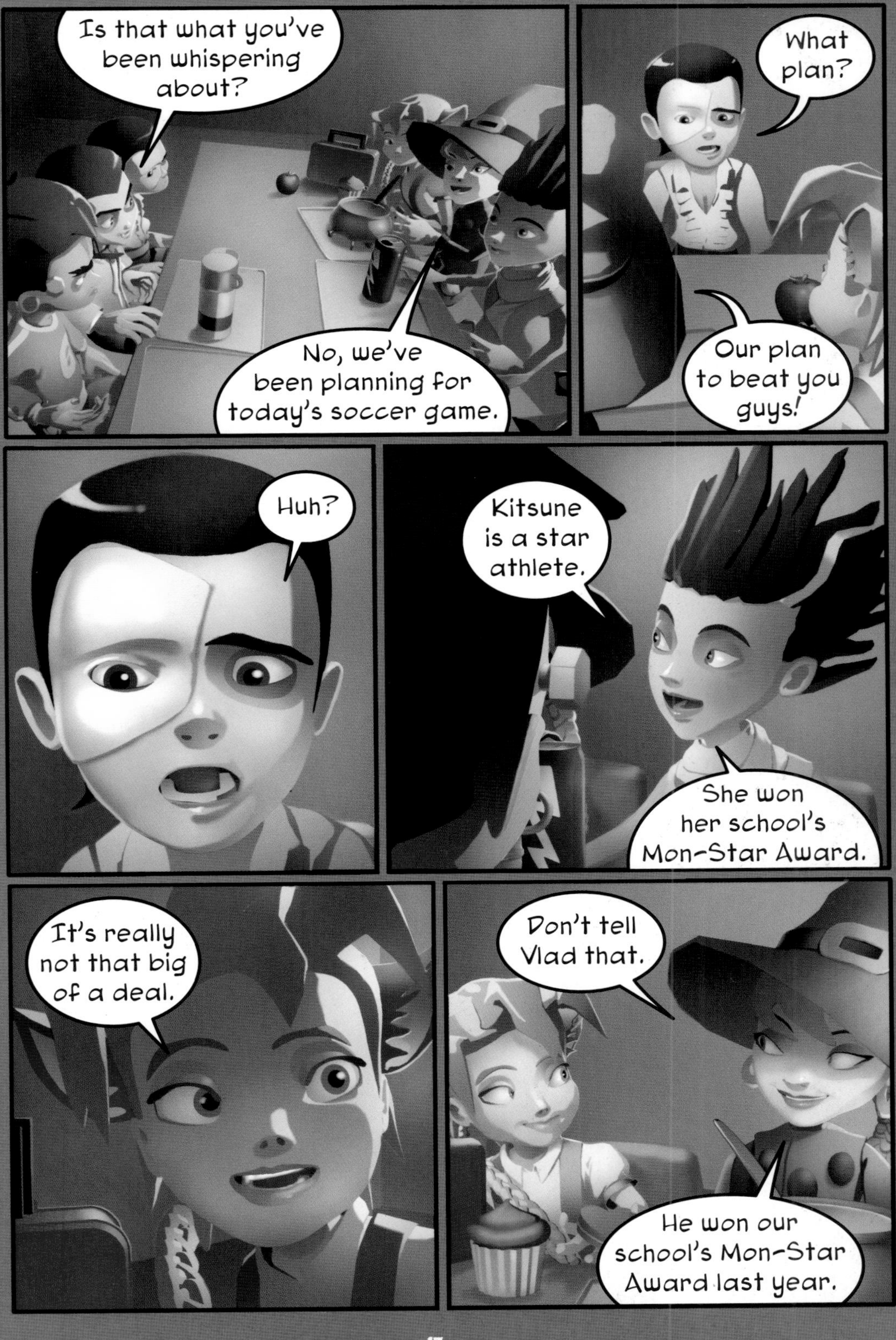
Is that what you've been whispering about?
No, we've been planning for today's soccer game.
What plan?
Our plan to beat you guys!
Huh?
Kitsune is a star athlete.
She won her school's Mon-Star Award.
It's really not that big of a deal.
Don't tell Vlad that.
He won our school's Mon-Star Award last year.

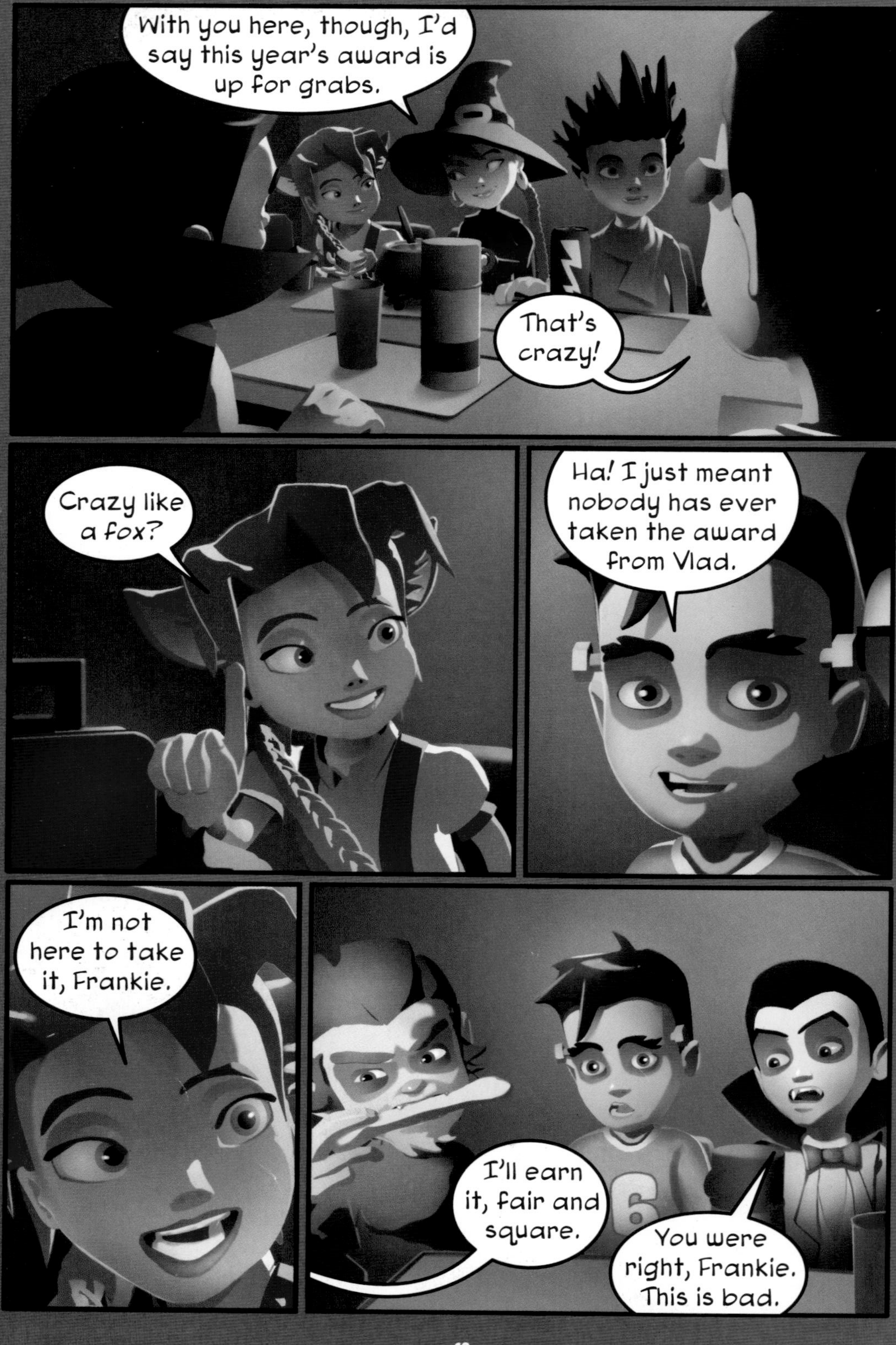
With you here, though, I'd say this year's award is up for grabs.
That's crazy!
Crazy like a fox?
Ha! I just meant nobody has ever taken the award from Vlad.
I'm not here to take it, Frankie.
I'll earn it, fair and square.
You were right, Frankie. This is bad.

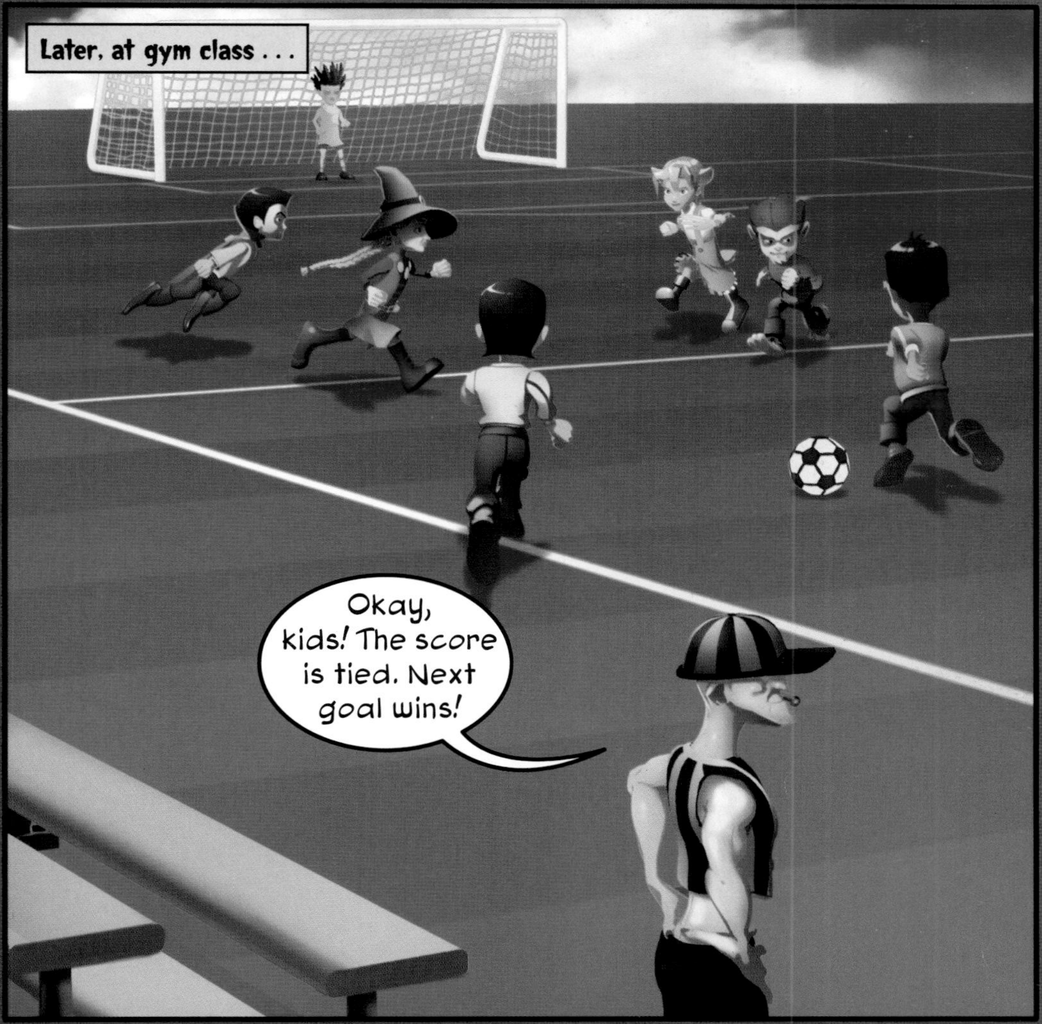
Later, at gym class . . .
Okay, kids! The score is tied. Next goal wins!

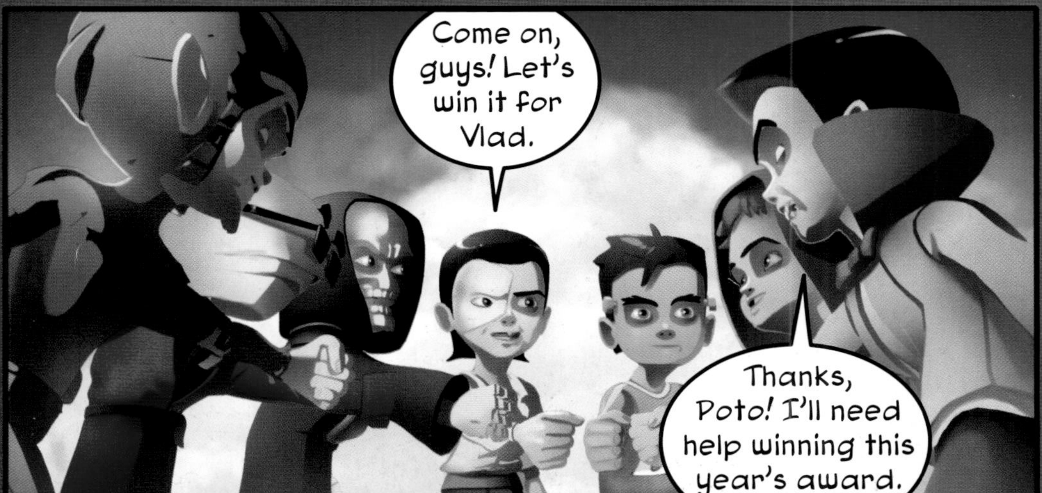
Come on, guys! Let's win it for Vlad.
Thanks, Poto! I'll need help winning this year's award.

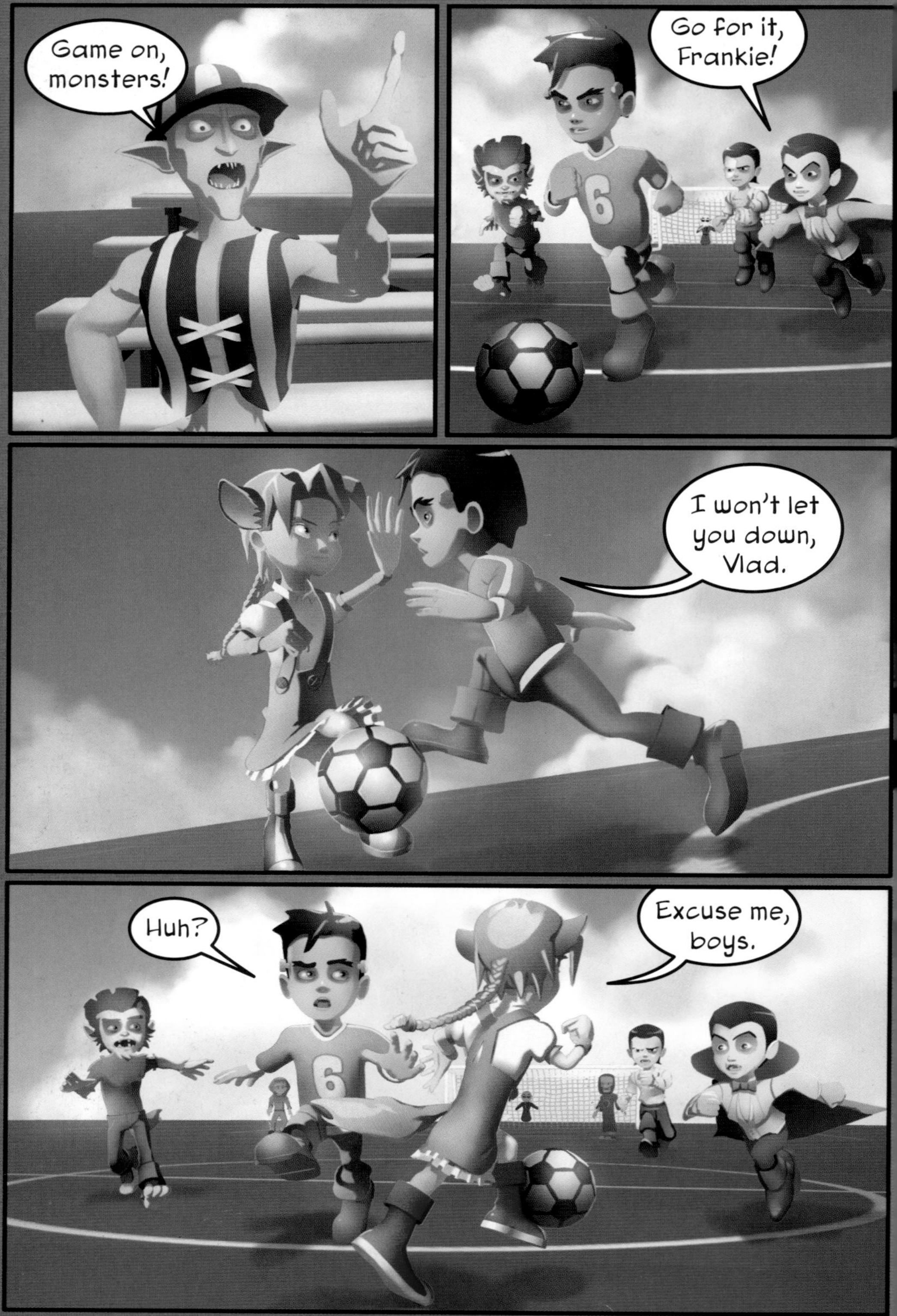
Game on, monsters!
Go for it, Frankie!
I won't let you down, Vlad.
Huh?
Excuse me, boys.

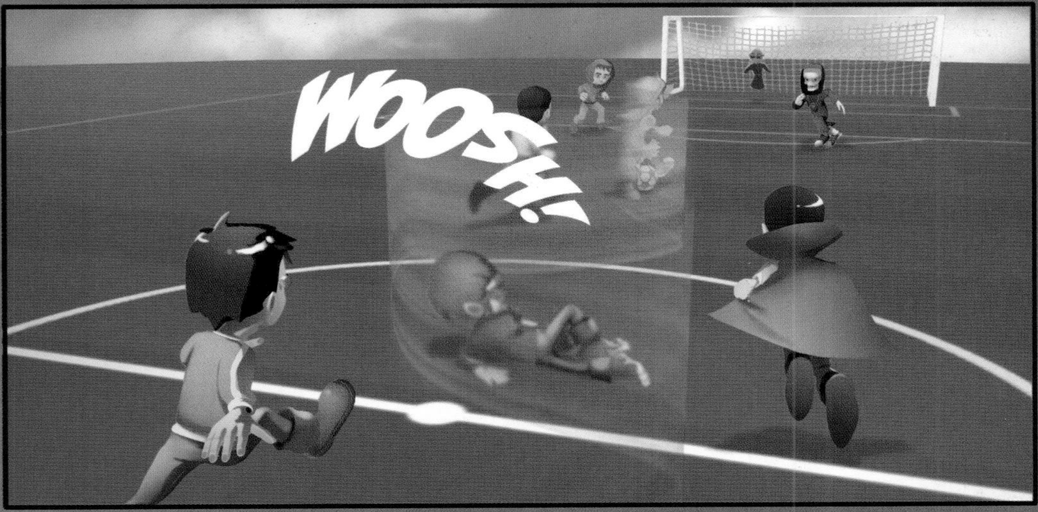
WOOSH!

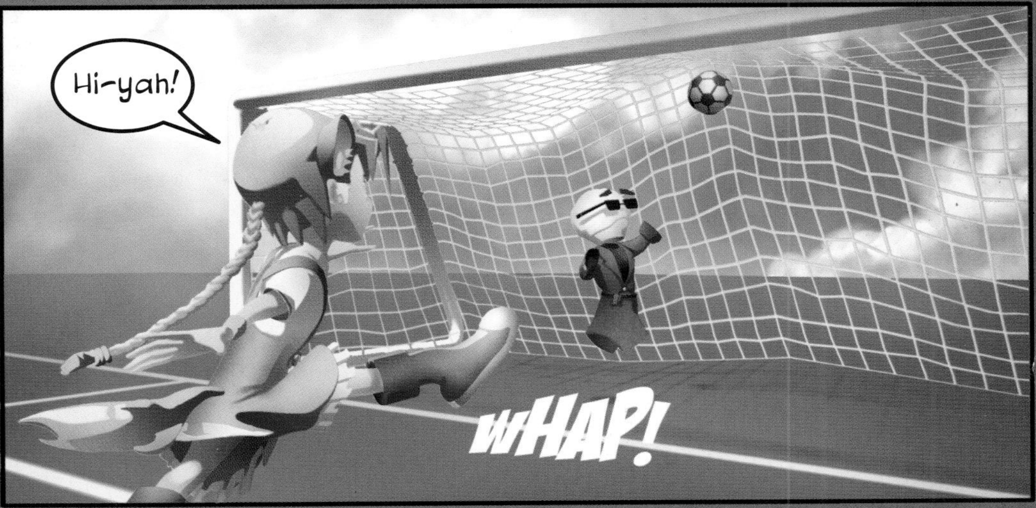
Hi-yah!
WHAP!

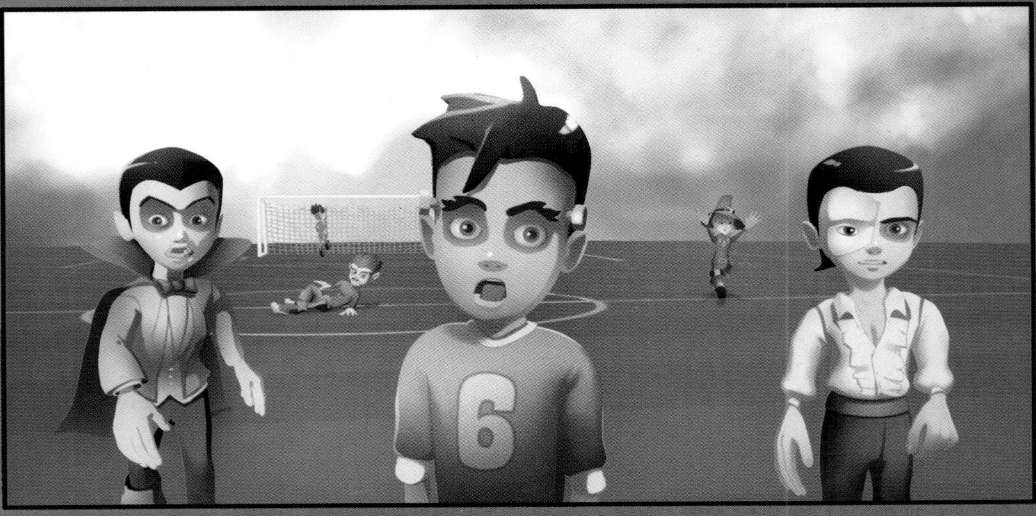

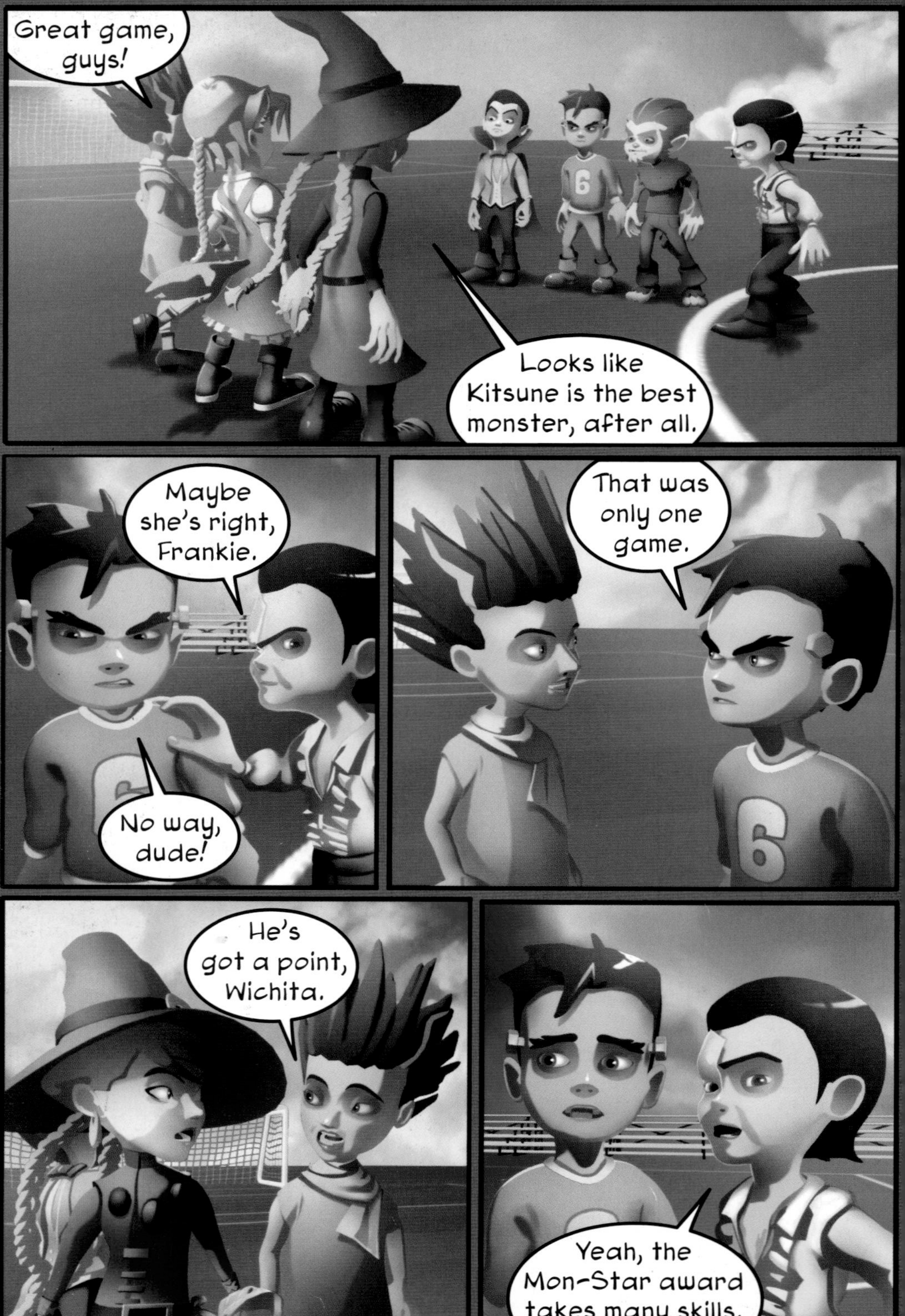
Great game, guys!
Looks like Kitsune is the best monster, after all.
Maybe she's right, Frankie.
No way, dude!
That was only one game.
He's got a point, Wichita.
Yeah, the Mon-Star award takes many skills.

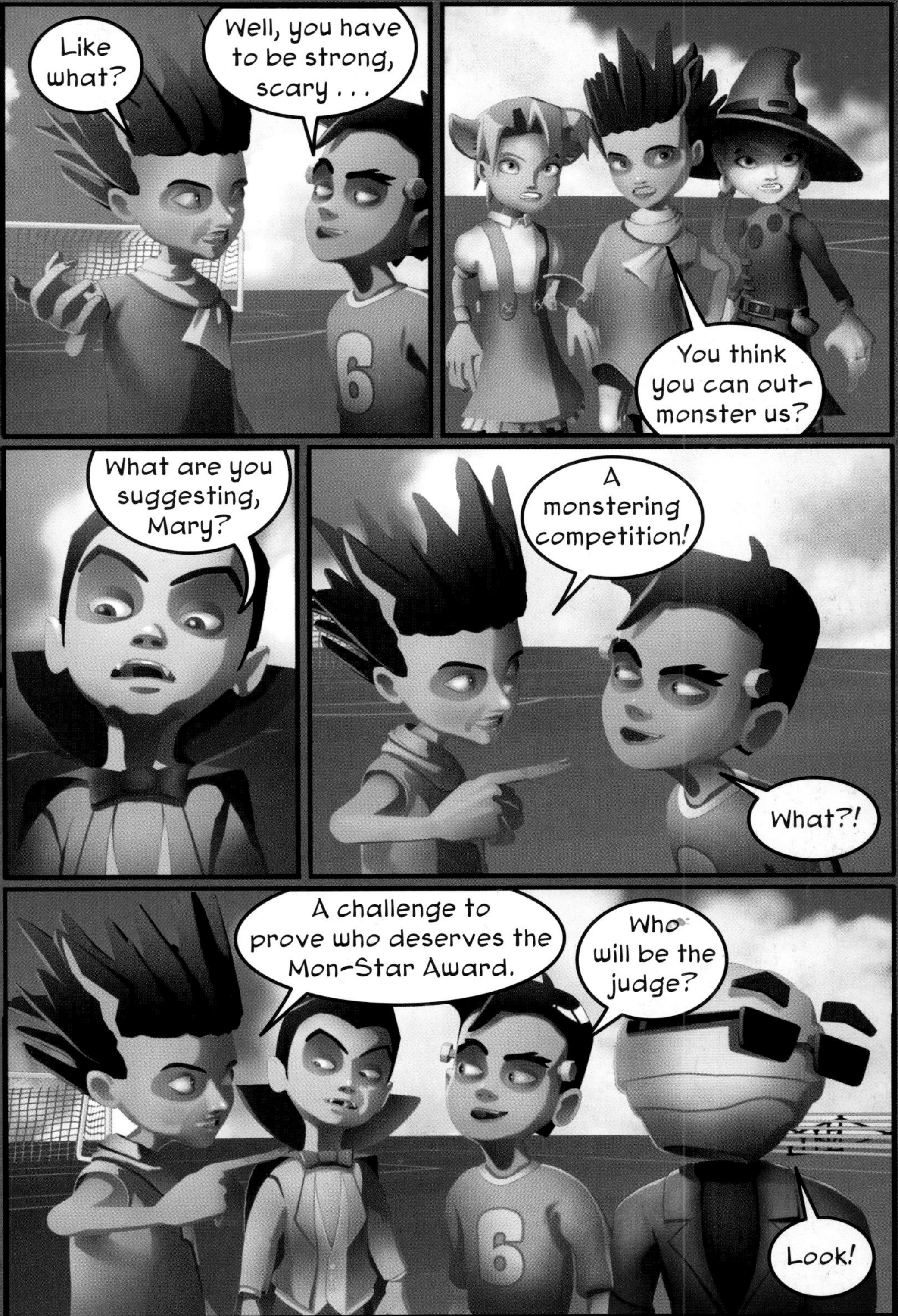

Like what?
Well, you have to be strong, scary . . .
You think you can out-monster us?
What are you suggesting, Mary?
A monstering competition!
What?!
A challenge to prove who deserves the Mon-Star Award.
Who will be the judge?
Look!

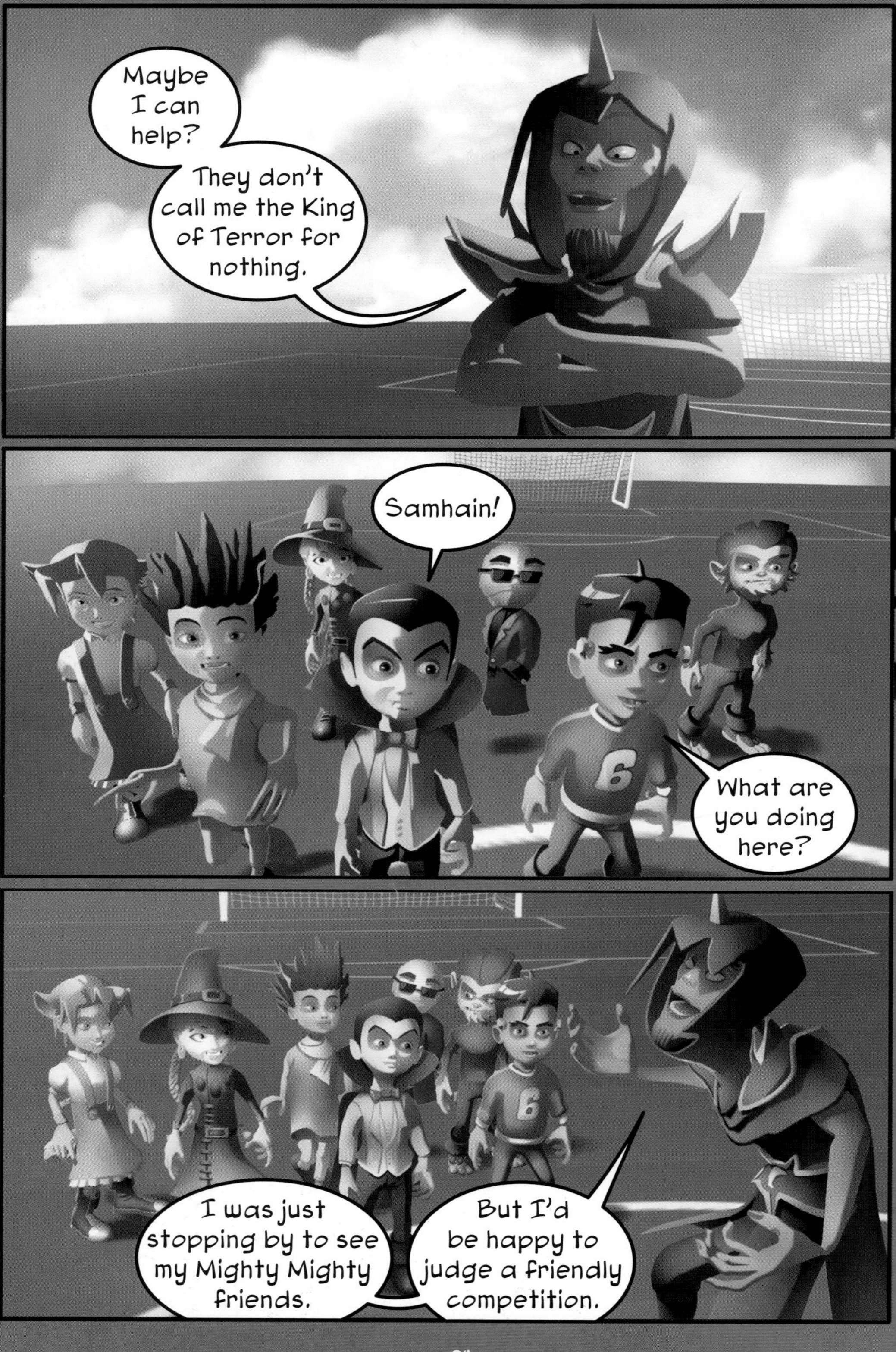
Maybe I can help?
They don't call me the King of Terror for nothing.
Samhain!
What are you doing here?
I was just stopping by to see my Mighty Mighty friends.
But I'd be happy to judge a friendly competition.

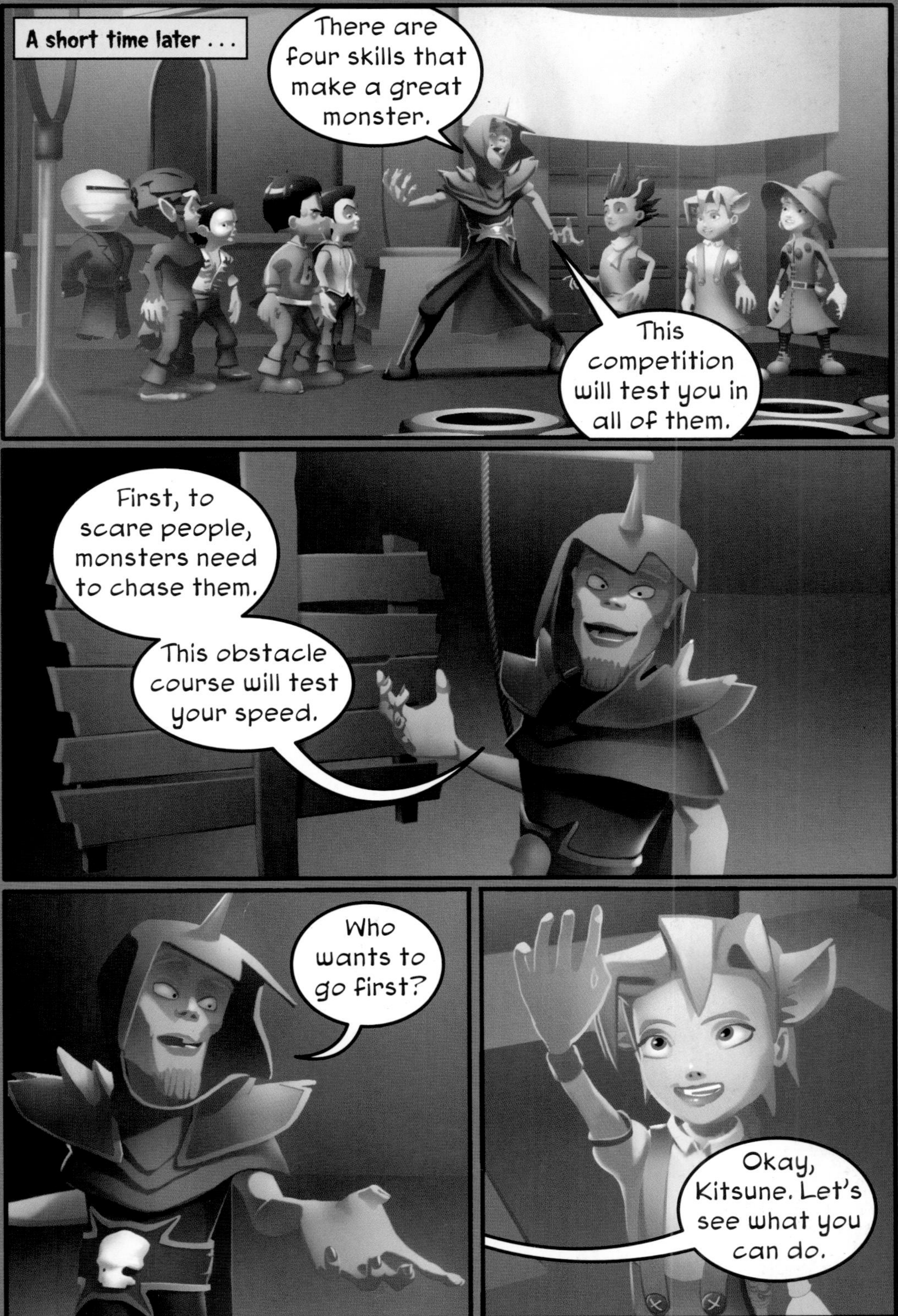
A short time later . . .
There are four skills that make a great monster.
This competition will test you in all of them.
First, to scare people, monsters need to chase them.
This obstacle course will test your speed.
Who wants to go first?
Okay, Kitsune. Let's see what you can do.

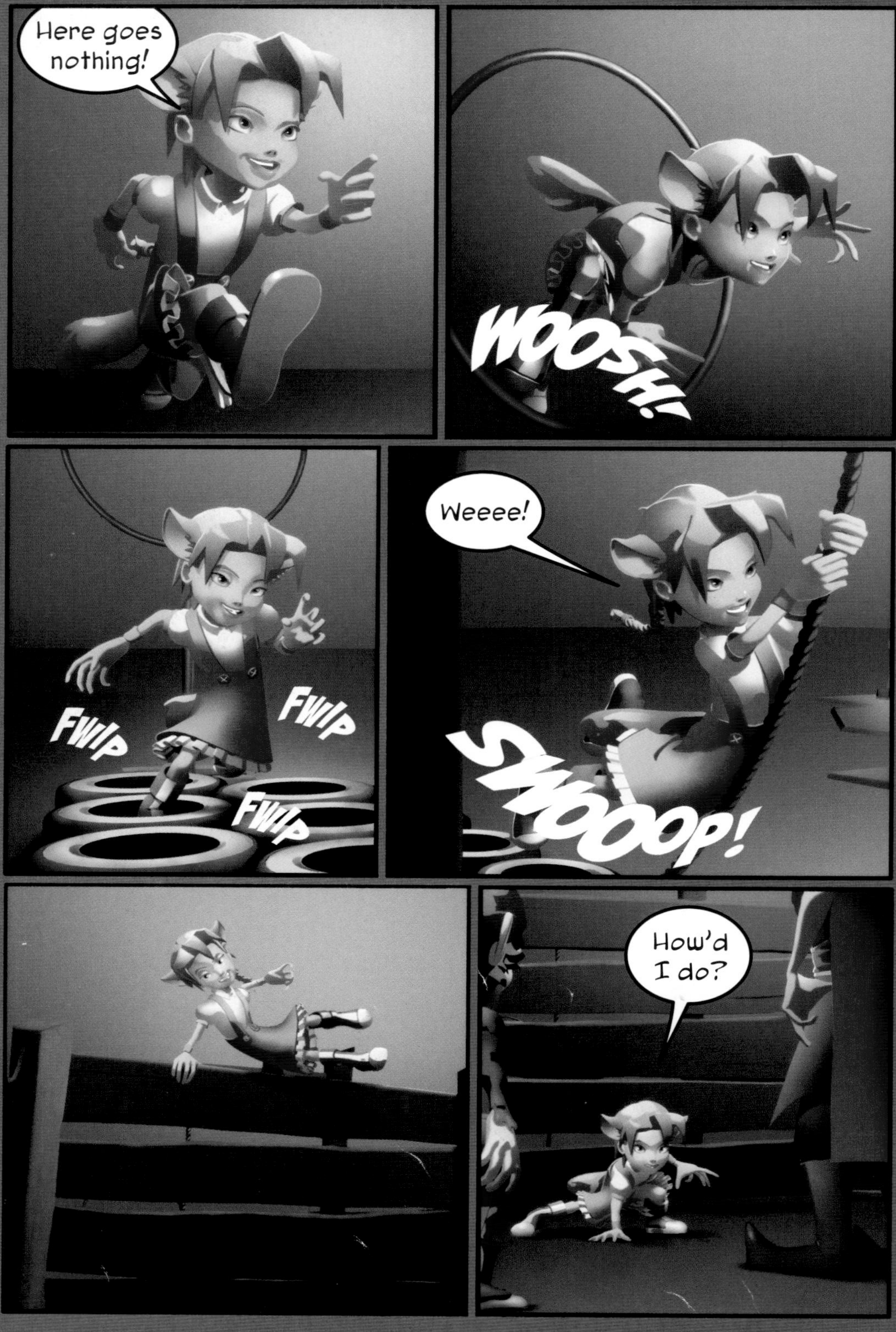
Here goes nothing!
WOOSH!
FWIP
FWIP
FWIP
Weeee!
SWOOOOP!
How'd I do?

Amazing!

I think you broke the course record.

Can I go next?

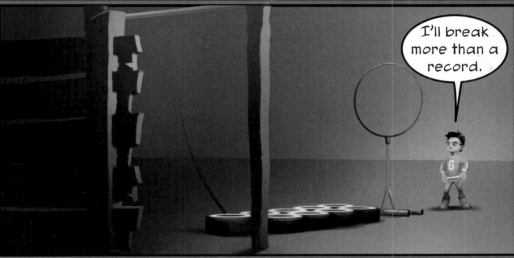

I'll break more than a record.

Okay, Frankie, but Kitsune's time will be tough to beat.

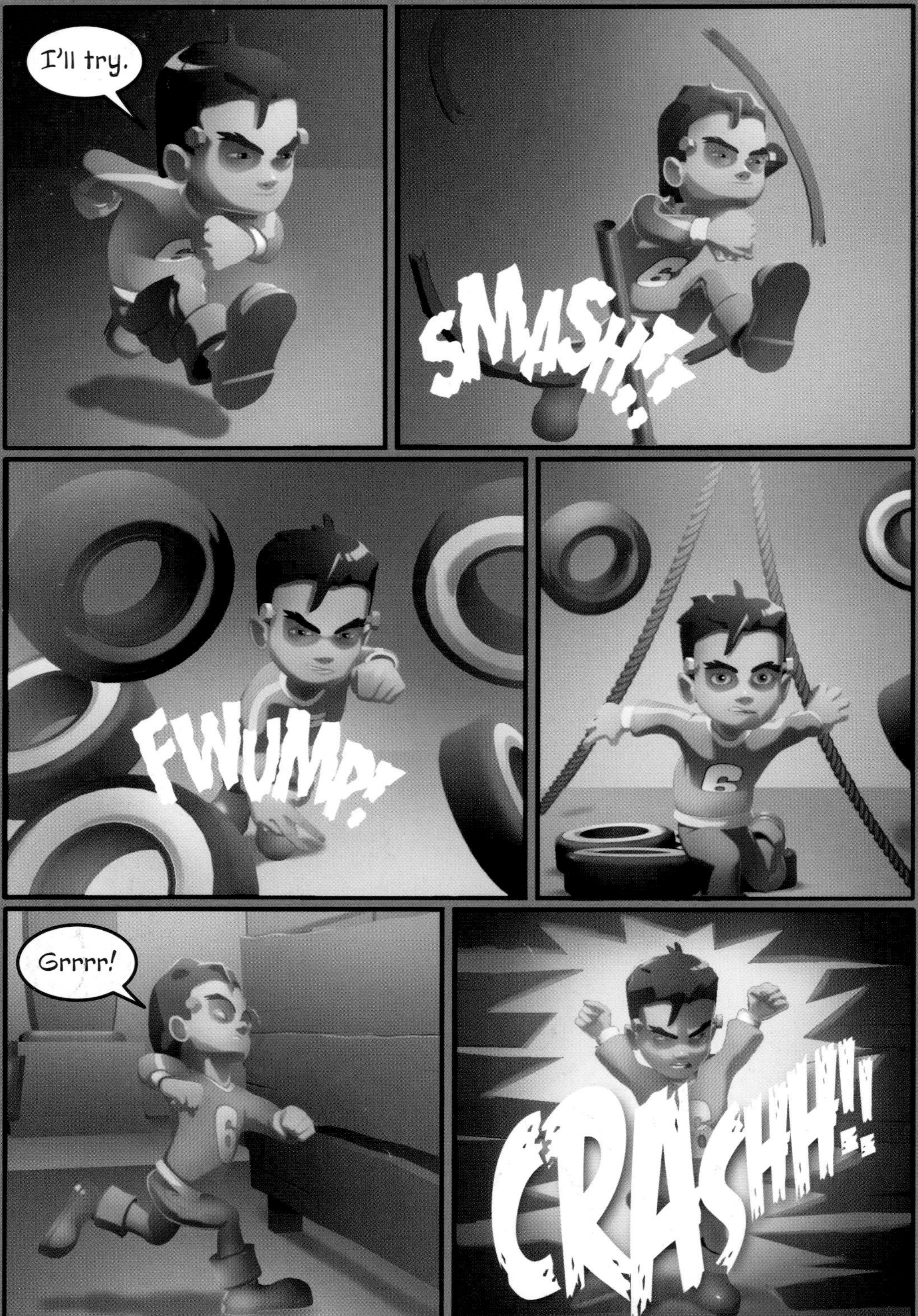
I'll try.
SMASH!!
FWUMP!
Grrrr!
CRASHH!!

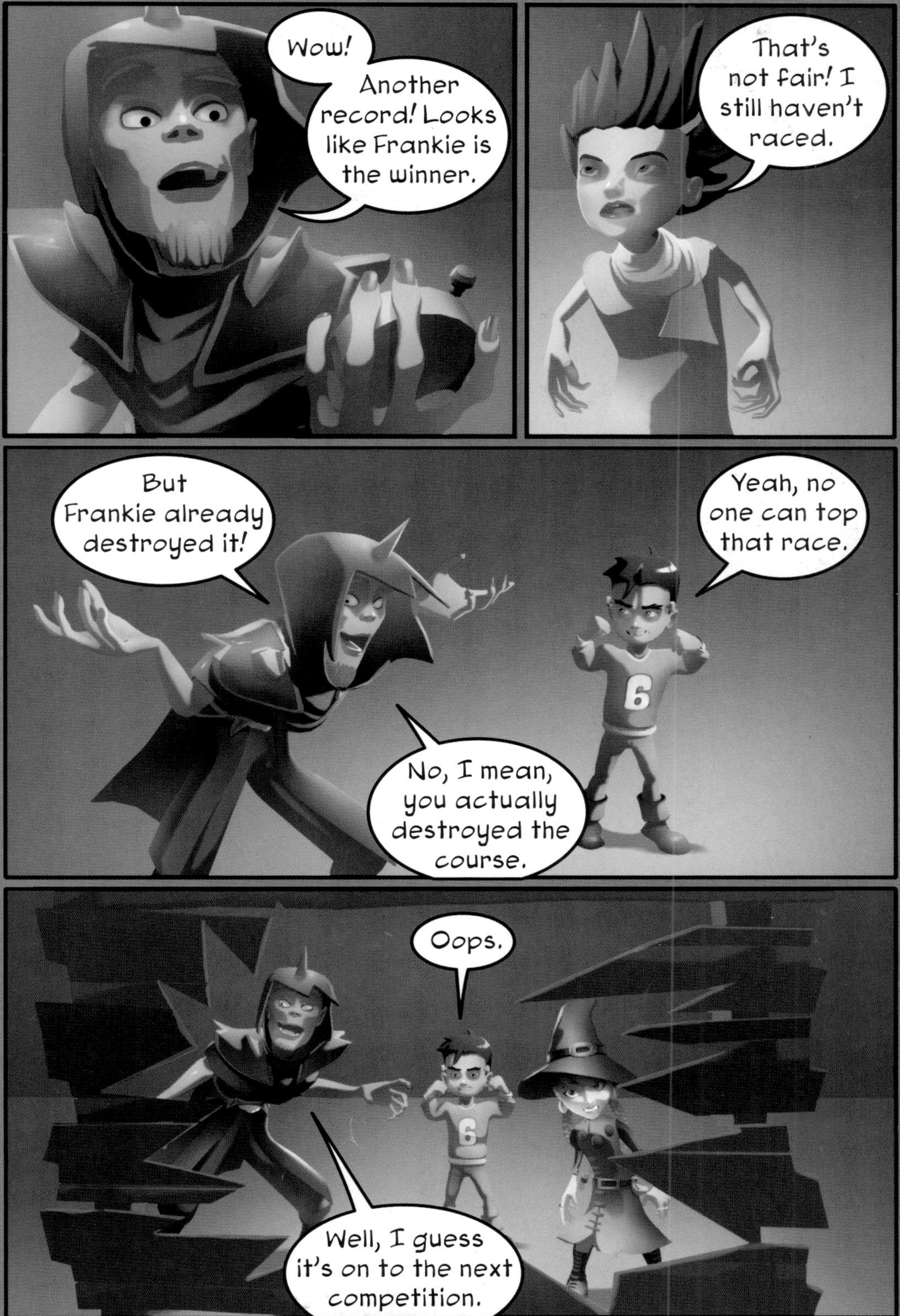
Wow! Another record! Looks like Frankie is the winner.
That's not fair! I still haven't raced.
But Frankie already destroyed it!
Yeah, no one can top that race.
No, I mean, you actually destroyed the course.
Oops.
Well, I guess it's on to the next competition.

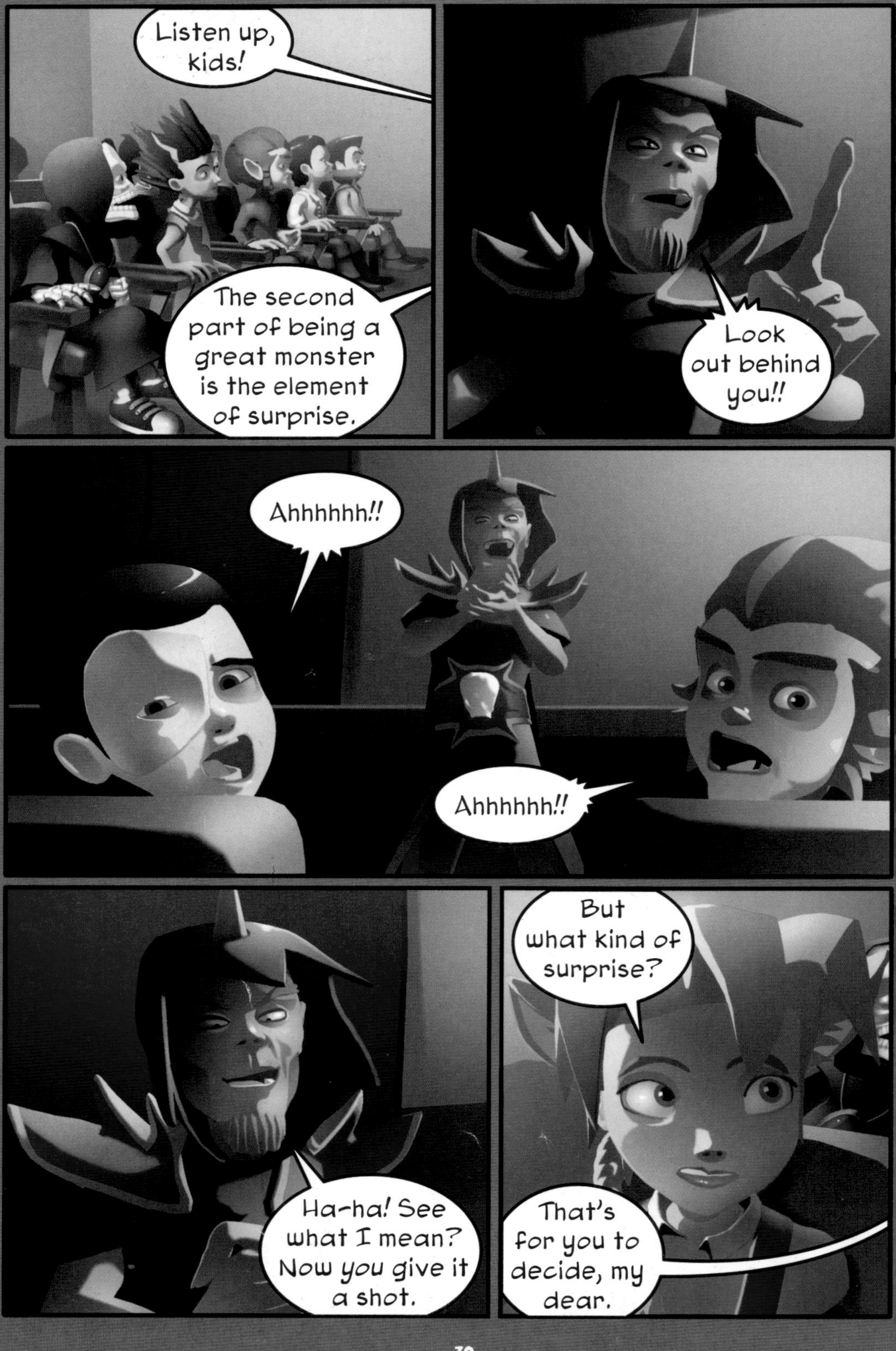
Listen up, kids!
The second part of being a great monster is the element of surprise.
Look out behind you!!
Ahhhhhh!!
Ahhhhhh!!
Ha-ha! See what I mean? Now you give it a shot.
But what kind of surprise?
That's for you to decide, my dear.

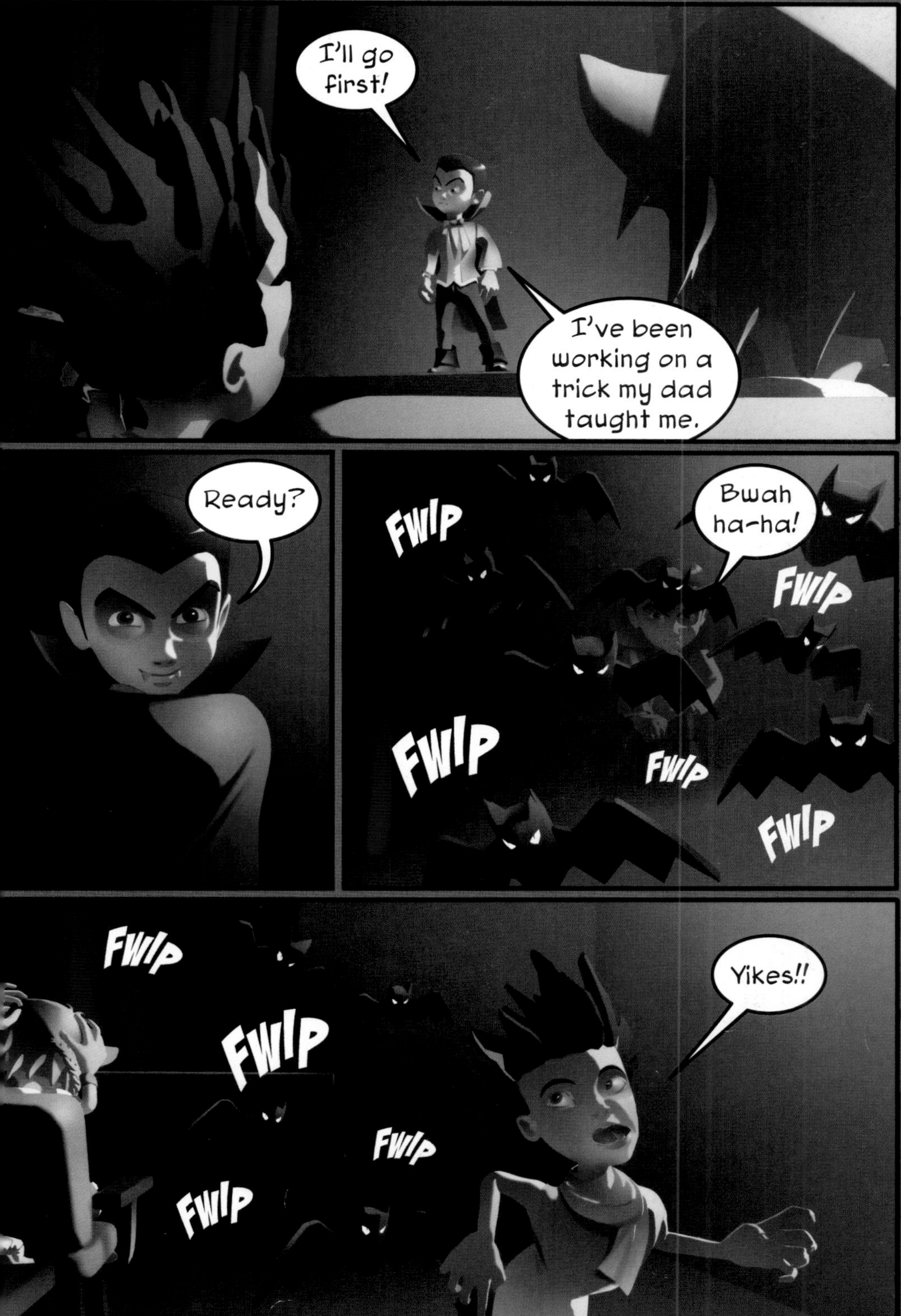
I'll go first!
I've been working on a trick my dad taught me.
Ready?
FWIP
Bwah ha-ha!
FWIP
FWIP
FWIP
FWIP
FWIP
Yikes!!
FWIP
FWIP
FWIP

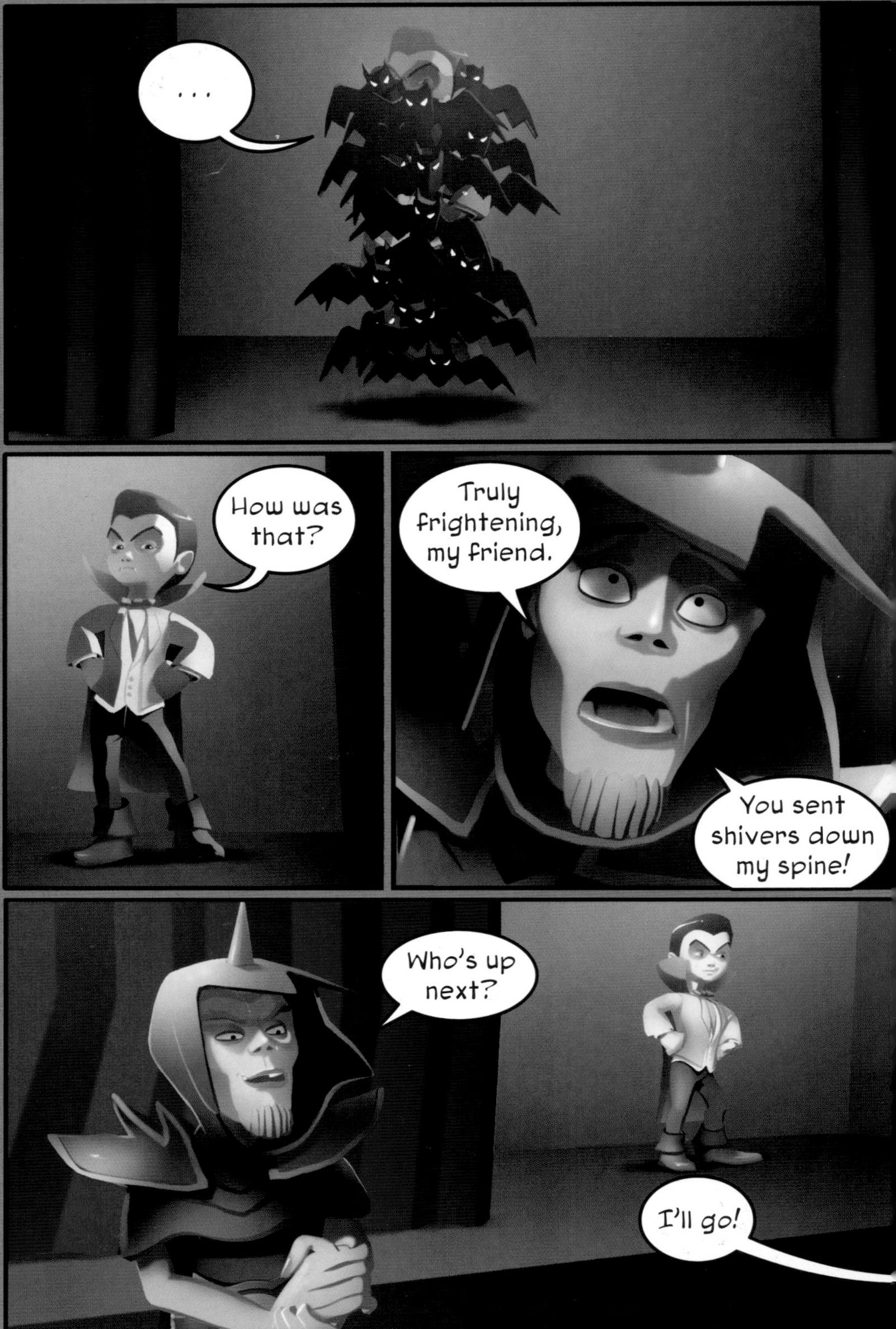
. . .
How was that?
Truly frightening, my friend.
You sent shivers down my spine!
Who's up next?
I'll go!

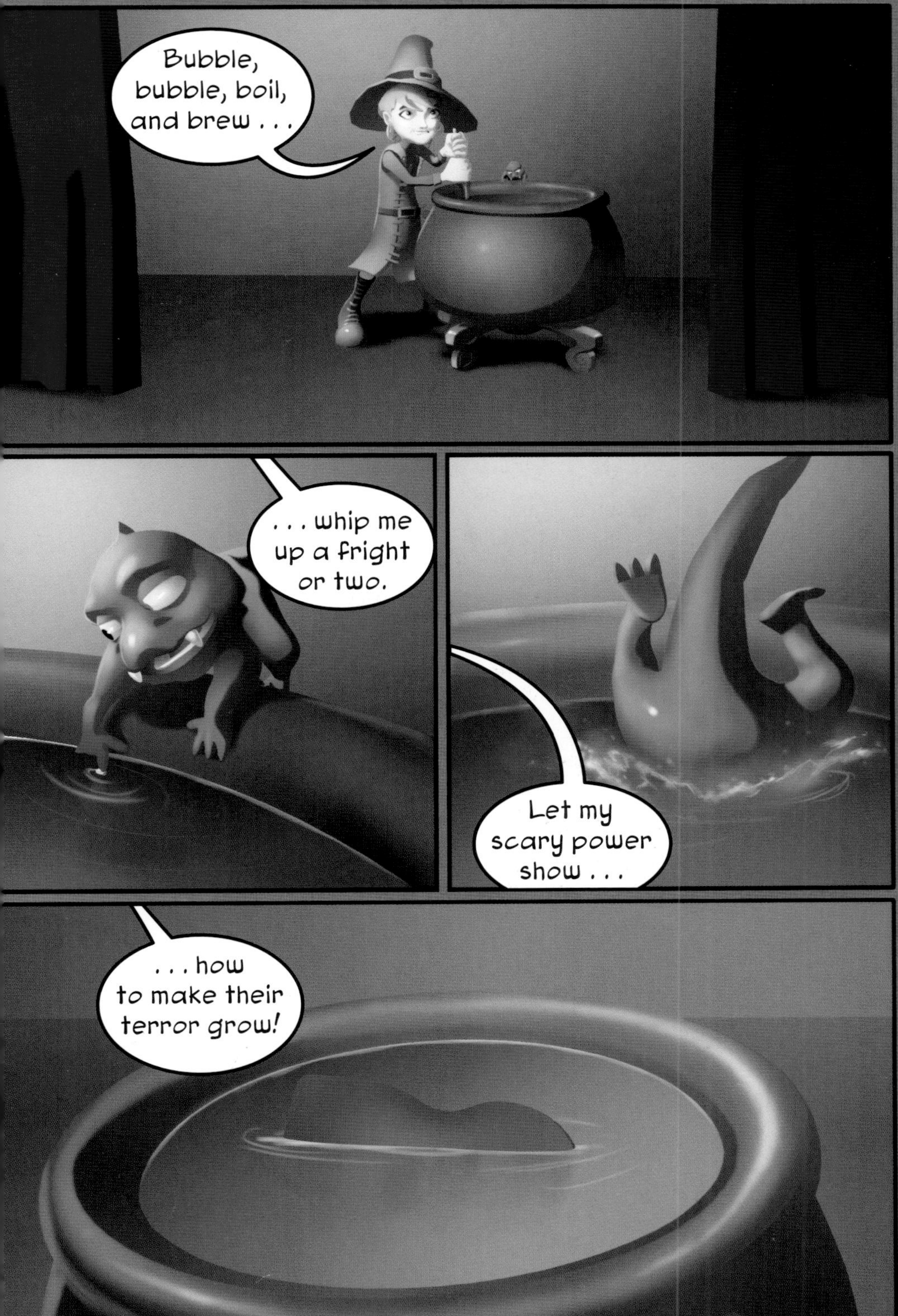
Bubble, bubble, boil, and brew . . .
. . . whip me up a fright or two.
Let my scary power show . . .
. . . how to make their terror grow!

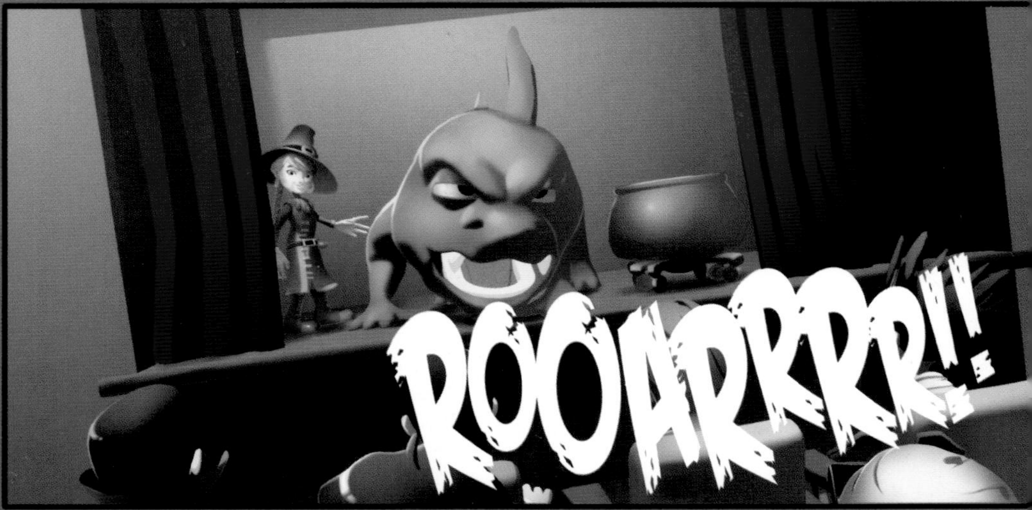
ROOARRRR!!

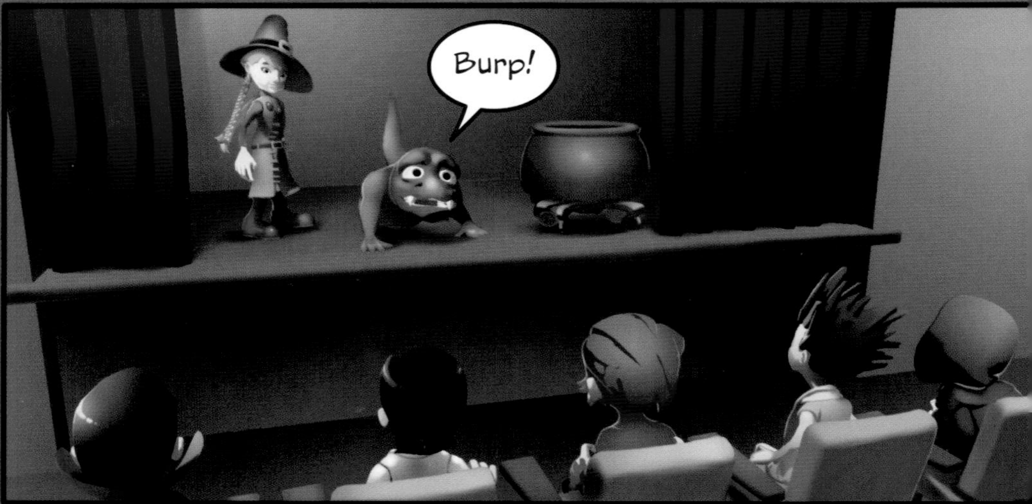
Burp!

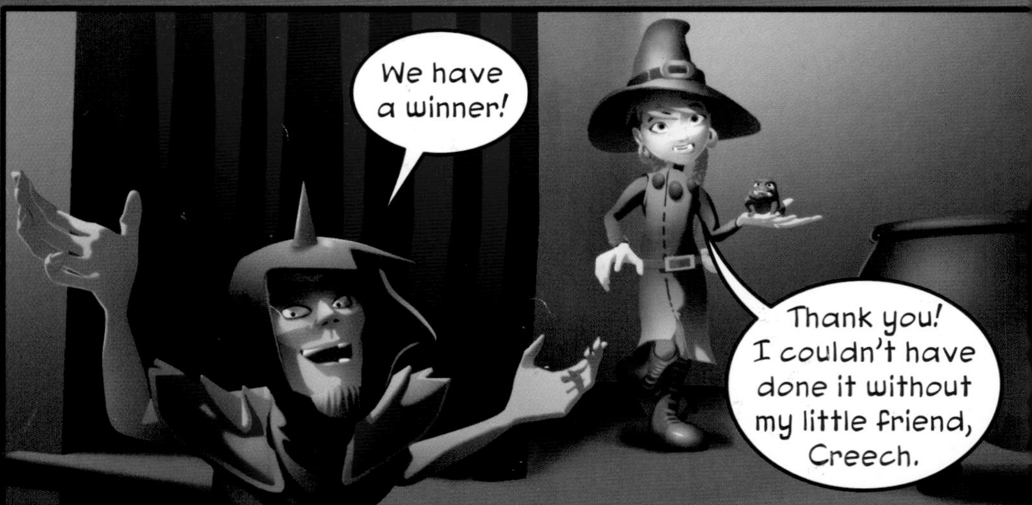
We have a winner!
Thank you! I couldn't have done it without my little friend, Creech.

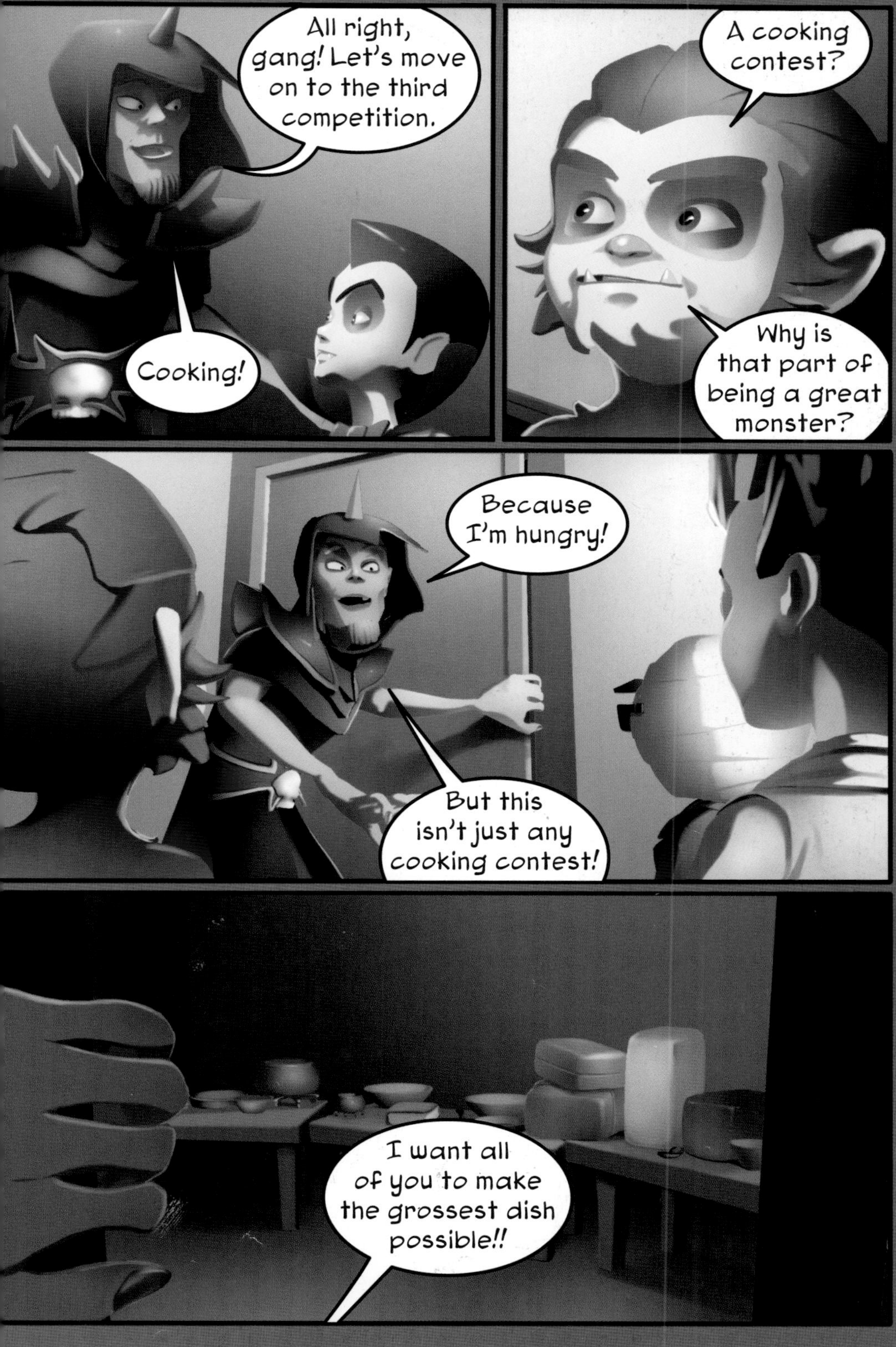
All right, gang! Let's move on to the third competition.
Cooking!
A cooking contest?
Why is that part of being a great monster?
Because I'm hungry!
But this isn't just any cooking contest!
I want all of you to make the grossest dish possible!!

One hour later . . .

Let's see what you all cooked up!

Want to try a little blood pudding?

Dog biscuits?

Electric eel cake?

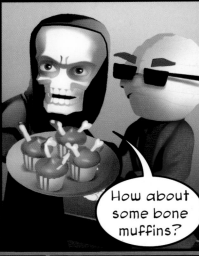

How about some bone muffins?

Puke pie?

Snot sauce?

Lizard legs?

Mmmm! Delicious.

So, who wins the Mon-Star Award?

There's one last skill every monster needs —

Yeah, tell us!

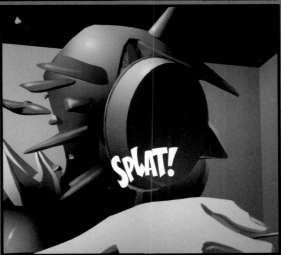

SPLAT!

Huh?

Monsters need to have fun too.

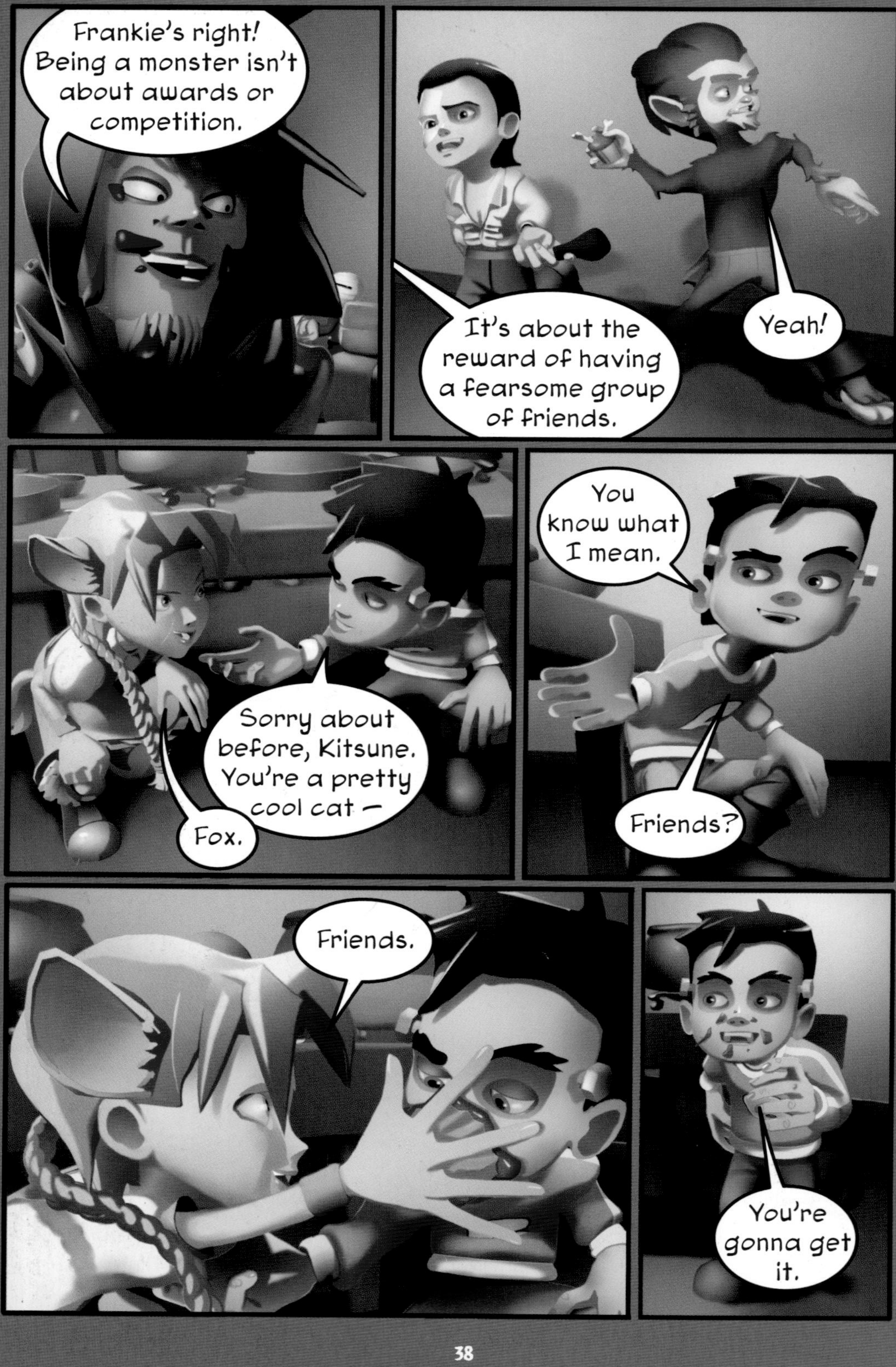
Frankie's right! Being a monster isn't about awards or competition.
It's about the reward of having a fearsome group of friends.
Yeah!
Sorry about before, Kitsune. You're a pretty cool cat —
Fox.
You know what I mean.
Friends?
Friends.
You're gonna get it.

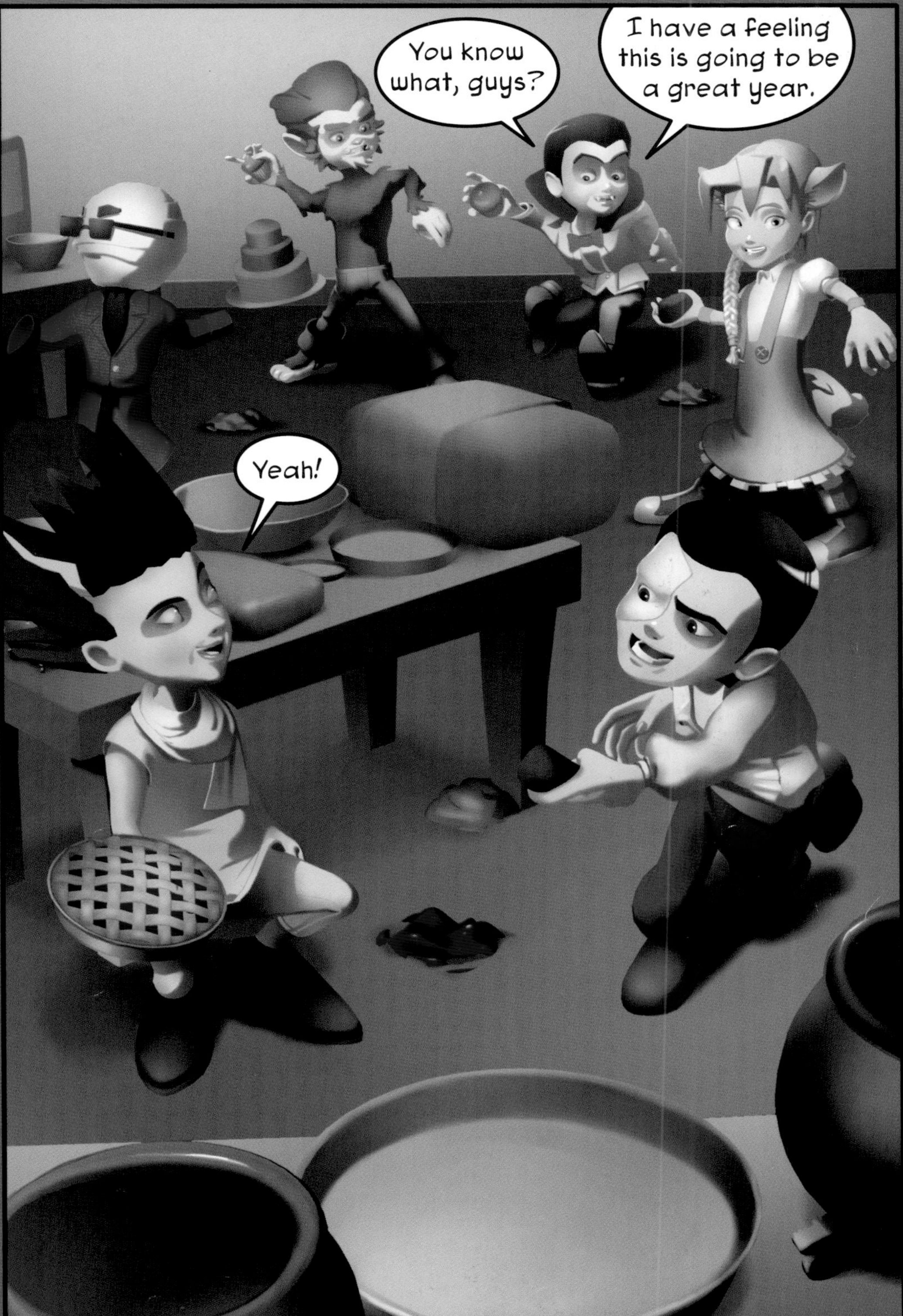
You know what, guys?
I have a feeling this is going to be a great year.
Yeah!

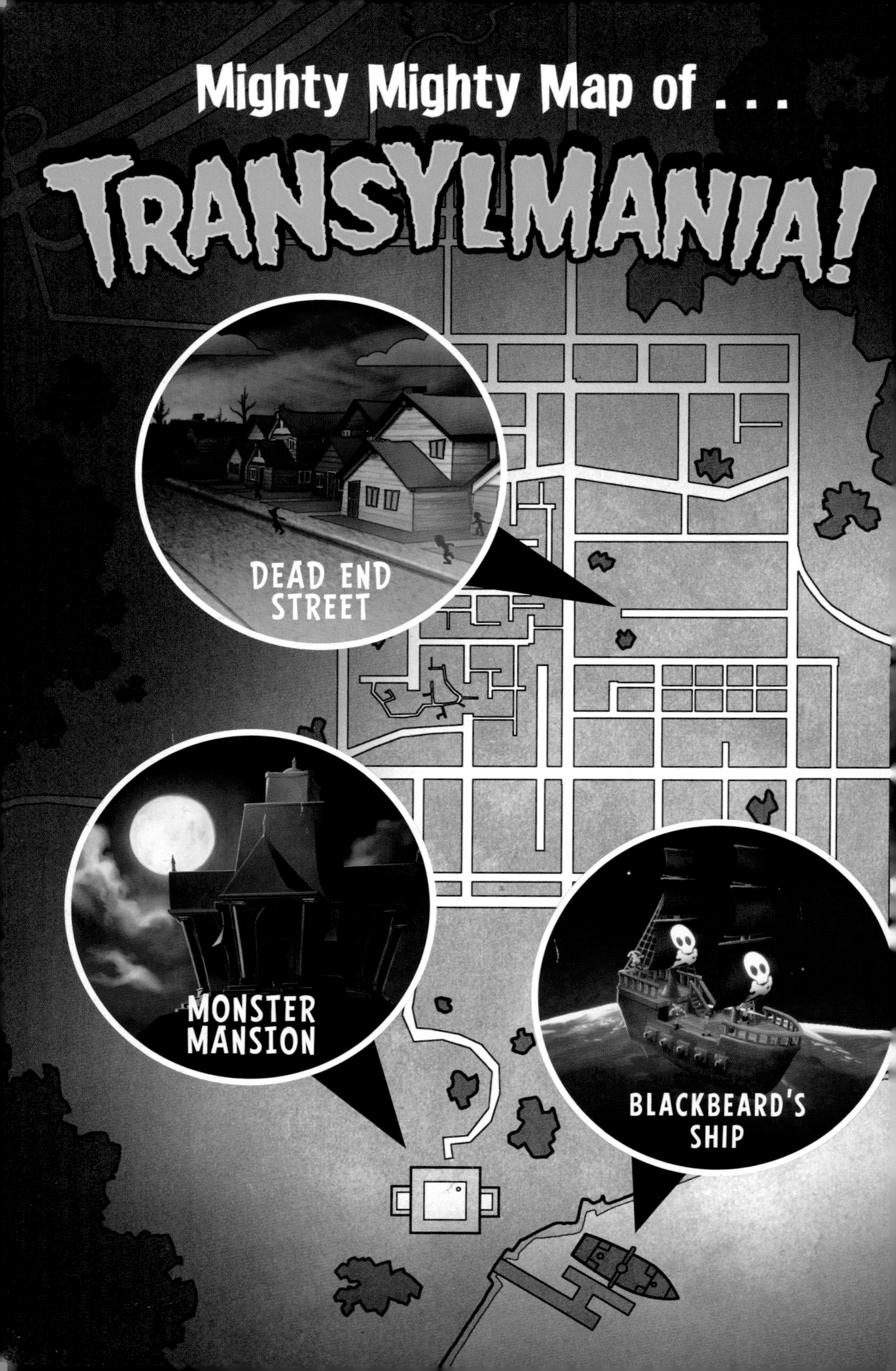
Mighty Mighty Map of . . .
TRANSYLMANIA!
DEAD END STREET
MONSTER MANSION
BLACKBEARD'S SHIP

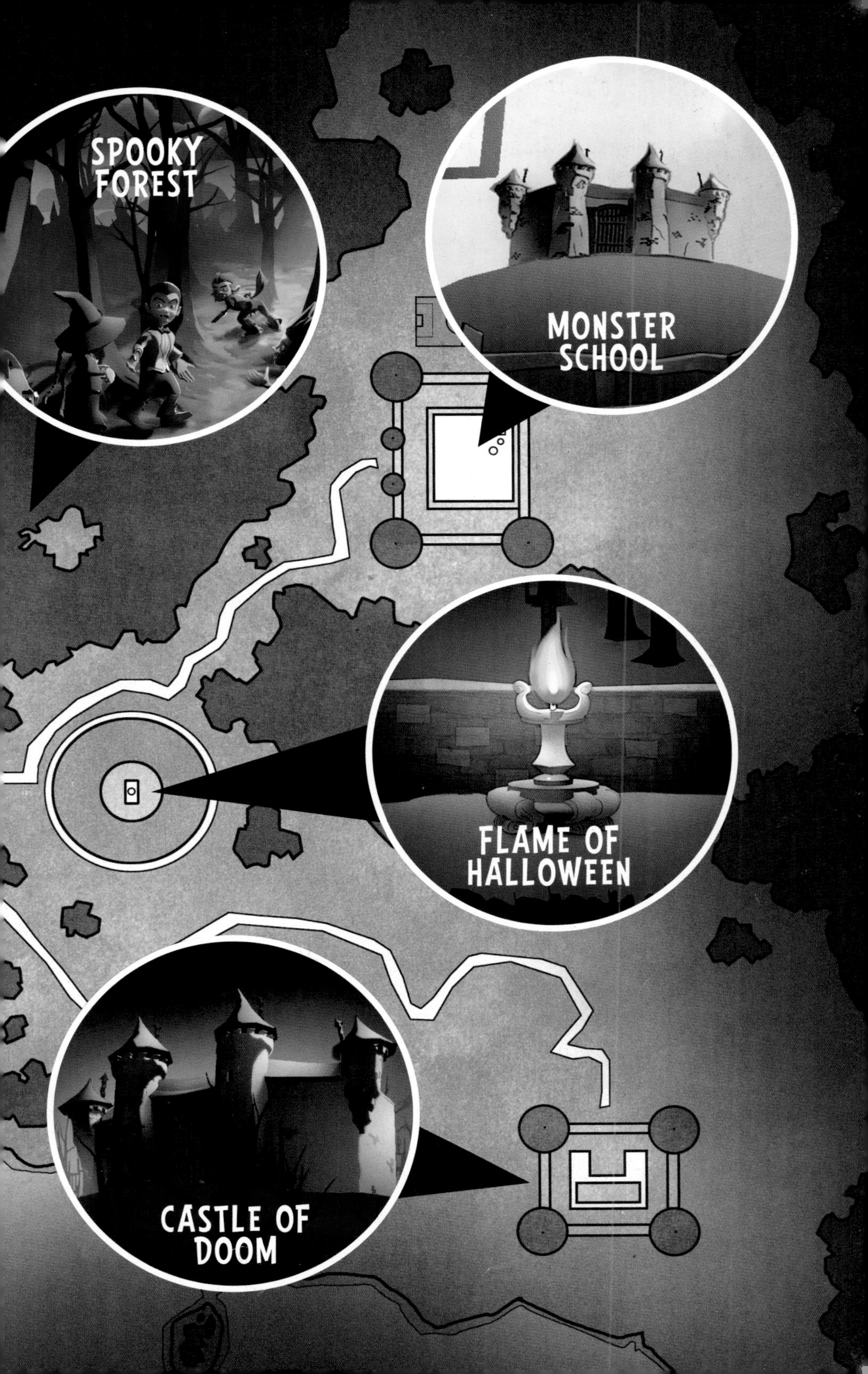
SPOOKY FOREST
MONSTER SCHOOL
FLAME OF HALLOWEEN
CASTLE OF DOOM

Mighty Mighty MONSTERS

...BEFORE THEY WERE STARS!

KITSUNE

Nickname: Kit

Hometown: Tokyo, Japan

Favorite Color: Pink

Favorite Animal: Foxes (of course!)

Mighty Mighty Powers: superhuman quickness on her feet; cleverness; extraordinary leaping ability; super friendliness.

BIOGRAPHY

Kitsune didn't grow up in Transylmania, but she quickly became an important member of the Mighty Mighty Monsters. Her speed and cleverness are unmatched. With her love for all things pink, she also adds a dose of "Girl Power" to the ghoulish gang. Although this fantastic fox is already a legend in her home country of Japan, she has made an instant impact on her new home.

In the country of Japan, *Kitsune* means fox. These clever animals have appeared in Japanese folklore for thousands of years.

In many folk tales, Kitsune creatures have magical powers and super intelligence. They can also have as many as nine tails. These tails show a Kitsune's age. A young fox might only have one, but an old fox could have many more.

Kitsune are famous for their cleverness. Oftentimes, they cannot be trusted and are considered greedy tricksters.

ABOUT SEAN O'REILLY
AND ARCANA STUDIO

As a lifelong comics fan, Sean O'Reilly dreamed of becoming a comic book creator. In 2004, he realized that dream by creating Arcana Studio. In one short year, O'Reilly took his studio from a one-person operation in his basement to an award-winning comic book publisher with more than 150 graphic novels produced for Harper Collins, Simon & Schuster, Random House, Scholastic, and others.

Within a year, the company won many awards including the Shuster Award for Outstanding Publisher and the Moonbeam Award for top children's graphic novel. O'Reilly also won the Top 40 Under 40 award from the city of Vancouver and authored *The Clockwork Girl* for Top Graphic Novel at Book Expo America in 2009.

Currently, O'Reilly is one of the most prolific independent comic book writers in Canada. While showing no signs of slowing down in comics, he now writes screenplays and adapts his creations for the big screen.

GLOSSARY

batty (BAT-tee)—crazy or insane

biscuit (BISS-kit)—a small, round bread, often made with baking soda

competition (kom-puh-TISH-shuhn)—a contest of some kind

destroyed (di-STROID)—wreck or ruined

fearsome (FIHR-suhm)—frightening, such as a monster

focus (FOH-kuhss)—to make something clearer to see with your eyes

introduce (in-truh-DOOSS)—to tell the name of one person to another person

Kitsune (kit-SOO-nee)—the Japanese word for fox, an animal often found in that country's folklore

locust (LOH-kuhst)—a type of grasshopper that eats and destroys crops

obstacle course (OB-stuh-kuhl KORSS)—a training course, which usually has fences, walls, and ditches to climb over or get around

terror (TER-uhr)—a person or thing that causes very great fear

DISCUSSION QUESTIONS

1. Why do you think the boy monsters didn't like Kitsune at first? Do you think they liked her at the end of the story? Explain.

2. Who do you think deserves the Mon-Star Award? Choose one monster and explain why he or she is the scariest.

3. All of the Mighty Mighty Monsters are different. Which character do you like the best and why?

WRITING PROMPTS

1. Have you ever been in a competition? Did you win or lose? Write a story about the game or event.

2. Write a story about your own group of friends. What kind of adventures do you have? What do you do for fun?

3. Write your own Mighty Mighty Monsters adventure. What will the ghoulish gang do next? What villains will they face? You decide.

Mighty Mighty MONSTERS ADVENTURES

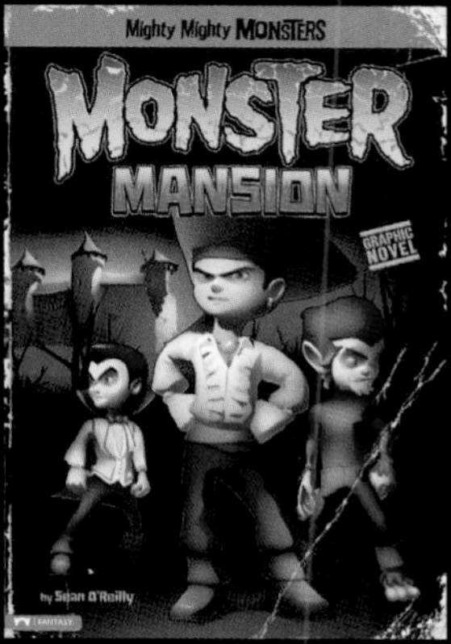
Mighty Mighty MONSTERS
MONSTER MANSION
GRAPHIC NOVEL
by Sean O'Reilly

Monster Mansion

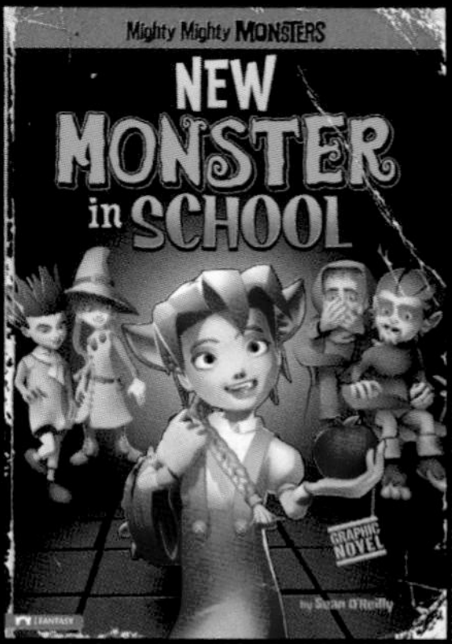
Mighty Mighty MONSTERS
NEW MONSTER in SCHOOL
GRAPHIC NOVEL
by Sean O'Reilly

New Monster in School

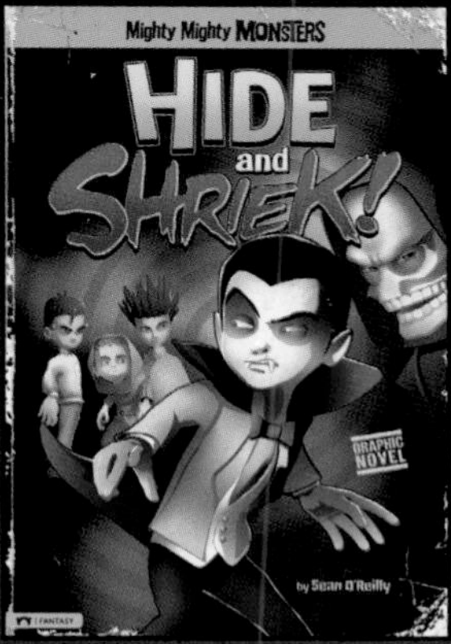
Mighty Mighty MONSTERS
HIDE and SHRIEK!
GRAPHIC NOVEL
by Sean O'Reilly

Hide and Shriek

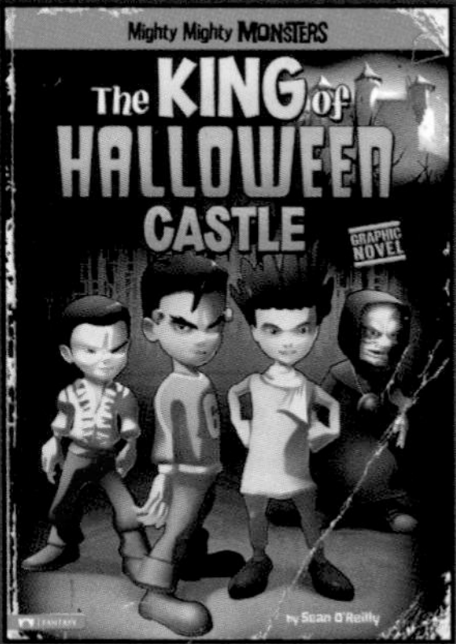
Mighty Mighty MONSTERS
The KING of HALLOWEEN CASTLE
GRAPHIC NOVEL
by Sean O'Reilly

The King of Halloween Castle

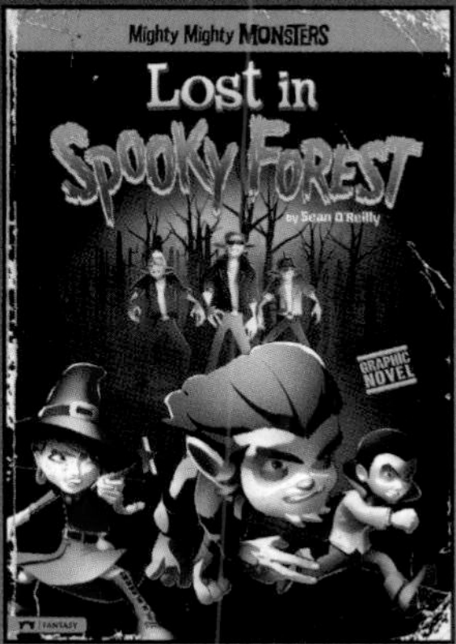
Mighty Mighty MONSTERS
Lost in Spooky Forest
by Sean O'Reilly
GRAPHIC NOVEL

Lost in Spooky Forest

WAIT!

DON'T CLOSE THE BOOK!

THERE'S MORE!

FIND MORE:

GAMES & PUZZLES
HEROES & VILLAINS
AUTHORS & ILLUSTRATORS

AT...

capstone kids.com

WWW.CAPSTONEKIDS.COM

STILL WANT MORE?

FIND COOL WEBSITES AND MORE BOOKS LIKE THIS ONE AT www.FACTHOUND.COM.
JUST TYPE IN THE BOOK ID: 9781434221513 AND YOU'RE READY TO GO!